"Look, Malcolm, for both of us."

"Awkward? Is that what this is?" Malcolm leaped to his feet, and she instinctively took a step back. "Awkward doesn't begin to define what this is. Why are you here?"

Lauren frowned and folded her arms. "I don't know what you mean."

"You could've taken a job anywhere. Why here?" he asked through clenched teeth. "I don't want you here."

She placed her hands on her hips and leaned up in his face, her dark brown eyes flashing with anger. "Because this is where I wanted to work. I was offered an opportunity few get, and taking it meant being closer to my family. What was I supposed to do, check with you first? News flash, Malcolm Gray, I don't need your permission for my job choice, and whether you like it or not, I plan to be here for a long time!"

Something within him snapped, and before his action registered in his brain, he hauled her into his arms and crushed his mouth against hers in a hungry and demanding kiss.

Dear Reader,

Well, self-proclaimed bachelor for life Malcolm Gray is the sole holdout of the Gray clan, or so he thinks, until his past shows up in the form of his college sweetheart, Lauren Emerson. If you've kept up with the Gray brothers, you know that they possess a chivalry gene. Malcolm is no different, which makes it hard to keep his distance. Lauren gives as well as she gets, and sparks fly. They both have regrets, but there's something sweet about love the second time around…if they're willing to risk it all.

I had a fabulous time writing Siobhan, Morgan, Brandon, Khalil and Malcolm's stories, and hope you enjoyed each of these siblings' journeys to happily-ever-after. Next up are their cousins, the Hunters of Sacramento, and I'm excited to introduce them to you.

As always, I so appreciate all your love and support. Without you, I couldn't do this.

Much love,

Sheryl

SherylLister.com

sheryllister@gmail.com

Facebook.com/SherylListerAuthor

Twitter.com/1Slynne

Instagram.com/sheryllister

Still Loving You

SHERYL LISTER

WITHDRAWN

(H) **HARLEQUIN**® KIMANI™ ROMANCE

Recycling programs
for this product may
not exist in your area.

ISBN-13: 978-1-335-21662-5

Still Loving You

Copyright © 2018 by Sheryl Lister

Printed in U.S.A.

Books by Sheryl Lister

Harlequin Kimani Romance

Visit the Author Profile page
atHarlequin.com for more titles.

For all those experiencing love the second time around.

Acknowledgments

My Heavenly Father, thank You for my life.
You never cease to amaze me with Your blessings!

To my husband, Lance, you continue to show me why
you'll always be my #1 hero!

To my children, family and friends, thank you for your
continued support. I appreciate and love you!

A special thank-you to my son-in-law, Otis Sutton, Sr.,
for the crash course in Madden (this story and *Places in
My Heart*). Love you so much!

To my Club N.E.O. sisters, I love you ladies!

A special thank-you to the readers and authors I've met
on this journey. You continue to enrich my life.

Thank you to my editor, Patience Bloom, for your
editorial guidance and support.

A very special thank-you to my agent, Sarah E. Younger.
I can't tell you how much I appreciate having you in my
corner.

Chapter 1

"Are you out of your *freaking* mind?"

Lauren Emerson paused in her packing and glanced over at her best friend sitting on the other side of the bed. "What? I just think it's time to move back home. I miss my family." She had moved to Phoenix from LA eight years ago to complete her master's in nutrition at Arizona State and stayed after being offered a job at the hospital where she had worked as an intern. Now she had a chance to go back to LA, and with a job that most people could only dream about.

Valencia Flores snorted. "Moving back home because 'I miss my family' is getting a nice job at a hospital or some other health center, *not* taking a job with the LA Cobras football team." She jumped up. "This is like…like *crazy*."

"Maybe so, but I can't pass up this opportunity."

"What do you think he's going to say when he walks in and sees you?"

Lauren resumed folding her shirts and placing them in

the open suitcase. "I don't know. It's been a long time, and I'm sure Malcolm has forgotten all about me."

Valencia stared at Lauren as if she had lost her mind. "A man does *not* forget the woman who broke his heart. Malcolm Gray loved you and you loved him. Everybody knew it. We were all just waiting for the wedding bells."

Lauren tossed the top in and blew out a long breath. She had been waiting for the same thing—until she made a foolish mistake. By the time she realized it, Lauren had ruined the best thing in she had going. "I'm sure there may be a few tense moments, but we're both adults and professionals. I plan to do my job and that's all. Not many people get the chance to be a nutritionist for a professional football team. And this will go a long way in giving me the credibility I need to write the book on nutrition for athletes."

Valencia folded her arms and angled her head thoughtfully. "Are you sure that's the only reason you're going?"

"Of course." Lauren had asked herself the same question several times over the three weeks since she'd accepted the position. Only yesterday had she finally admitted that a small part of her wanted to see Malcolm again. As a football fan, she had followed his career, and she was happy he'd been able to live the life they had talked about all those years ago. Back then, they would lie together laughing, talking and sharing their hopes and dreams.

"I hope you know what you're doing."

She glanced up to see Valencia still frowning. "I do. I'm taking advantage of an opportunity of a lifetime, and I'll be near my family. It's a win-win situation for me. How can that be a bad thing?" She had found a condo in Carson, a twenty-minute drive from her parents' house, which was far enough to maintain her privacy. The modern two-bedroom end unit had an open floor plan, granite countertops in the kitchen, hardwood flooring, a separate dining room, a two-car garage with direct access to the home, a balcony and a spacious master bedroom. And although it wasn't gated, there was twenty-four-hour security. A bonus was that the Cobras' practice facility was only about thirty minutes away.

Valencia viewed Lauren skeptically. "Okay, if you say so. Since you follow football, do you know if Malcolm is married or dating someone?"

Lauren walked over to her dresser, opened a drawer and grabbed another armful of clothing. "I follow *football*, not his personal life, so I have no idea." Malcolm had always been a private person when it came to his relationships, even when they dated. As a popular athlete at UCLA, he had been interviewed on a number of occasions. Whenever questions came up about his relationship with Lauren, Malcolm would give the standard "no comment" and shift the conversation back to football. Lauren did remember seeing a picture of him with a beautiful actress floating around on social media a year or two ago, with speculation about whether the two were headed to the altar. However, she never heard anything more, so she assumed it hadn't happened. She'd seen notices of his siblings' weddings, including that of his twin sister, Morgan. Lauren hadn't been the least bit surprised that Morgan had married a football star and had a successful career as a sports agent. The woman was a bigger fan of the game than Lauren. "So, you are coming to visit me soon, right?"

"Heck, yeah. I've only been to LA twice, so get ready to party." Valencia snapped her fingers and did a little dance step. "I'm going to be putting in for some time off as soon as I get in to work on Monday. Do you think the team needs another nutritionist? I mean…there's, like, how many on the team?"

"Usually about fifty-three."

"See, that's plenty for two people." She wiggled her eyebrows. "With all those fine muscular men in one place, I might learn to like football a little more."

Lauren laughed. "You're a hot mess." But her friend was

right. The LA Cobras were an impressive team. In more ways than one. She zipped the full suitcase and dragged it off the bed until it stood upright on its wheels. She set it next to the other two and glanced around the room at all the luggage and boxes stacked against the walls. It was a good thing she had ended her job two days ago. No way she would have finished packing everything otherwise. She hated moving. Somehow she had accumulated enough stuff over the past eight years to open her own variety shop. Clearly, she would have to go through her things after getting settled in her new place. "I really appreciate you taking today off to help me."

"You know I couldn't let you do all this alone. Besides, I haven't taken off one day this year, and we're already at the halfway mark." Valencia taped a box closed. "What time is the moving truck coming tomorrow?"

"Five in the morning," she answered with a groan. "The drive is supposed to be close to six hours, but with traffic, who knows?"

"Are you sure you don't want me to drive with you? I could stay overnight and hop a flight back on Sunday."

She stared at her best friend and seriously considered her offer. Lauren hated driving, and having someone with her would make the time go by faster. "Truthfully, I'd rather not drive by myself. You sure you wouldn't mind?"

Valencia rolled her eyes. "Of course I wouldn't mind. That's why I offered two weeks ago when you first told me."

Lauren chuckled. "I appreciate you, girl. It'll be easier if you just stay here tonight."

"I agree." Valencia finished taping another box. "Let me tape up these last two boxes and I'll run home, pack a bag and be back. Do you want me to stop and pick up something for dinner?"

"Seeing as how I've packed up all the dishes and cleaned

out the refrigerator, that might be a good idea. Maybe pizza? That's quick and doesn't require utensils."

"That works." The other woman picked up her purse and dug her keys out of her pocket. "Are you sure this is what you want to do, Lauren?"

Lauren knew Valencia wasn't asking about the job. "Yes." At best, she and Malcolm could come to some sort of truce—she'd do her job and he'd do his. At worst, he could still hate her guts and make her dream job a living nightmare.

Malcolm Gray finished his last set on the bench press, then moved so his brother-in-law Omar Drummond and another teammate, Marcus Dupree, could take their turns. All three men played for the LA Cobras, and although training camp didn't start until next month, everyone had been summoned for a Monday morning meeting. They decided to make good use of the time by arriving early and getting in a workout.

"I think I might be done when my contract is up," Marcus said, lying on the bench and starting his repetitions. "This body is getting too old for all those hits."

Omar nodded his head in agreement. "No lie."

Malcolm chuckled. "I hear you. Sometimes I feel like I'm going on sixty instead of thirty." While both Marcus and Omar started at the wide receiver position, Malcolm was the team's running back, and the punishment his body took week after week could be grueling. "My contract is up at the end of the season, and my agent is trying to get me to go for four more. I'm drawing the line at two, if that."

Marcus pushed the bar up and grunted. "You'll be what? Thirty?"

"Thirty-two by then." When he retired, he planned to join his brother Khalil's business. Maximum Burn Fitness Center had two locations that were currently doing well. They had discussed opening a third one within the next two years if the centers continued to run successfully. Though Malcolm had never imagined doing anything other than football, he was realistic enough to know he wouldn't be able to play forever. His family owned a home-safety company that manufactured everything from bath rails and specialized mattresses to in-home alert systems that let a person know if a door had been left open or a stove left on and detected human movement and sent the information to a smartphone. But the idea of wearing a suit and sitting behind a desk for the rest of his life like his brother Brandon and sister Siobhan held no appeal. Instead, he'd followed in Khalil's footsteps and earned a degree in kinesiology, which would give him options other than a desk.

Omar did a final set and moved to another machine. "You know I'm done when my contract is up. School is kicking my butt." He was halfway through his doctoral study program in clinical psychology and planned to join the staff of the veterans' mental health center he had co-founded. "What about you, Dupree? What are your plans?"

"Most likely physical therapy, since that's what my degree is in. I haven't decided whether I want to jump into academia or work in the field." He had completed his clinical doctorate in physical therapy two years ago.

They moved from machine to machine, perfectly executing the movements while continuing the conversation about their postfootball plans.

As they finished, another player approached. "Hey, you guys might want to hurry up and get to the auditorium. I heard the new nutritionist is a woman and she's *fine*! I'll be sitting front and center. Gotta get my eating program together." He hurried off.

Malcolm, Omar and Marcus shook their heads. The previous nutritionist had been fired at the end of last season when management got wind of him fudging the numbers on players who were in danger of losing their starting positions because they were overweight. Two players had been released during the controversy as well.

By the time they showered and made it to the auditorium, the room was abuzz with speculation.

"I'm so glad to be out of the dating game," Omar said with a chuckle. He and Malcolm's twin sister, Morgan, had married two years ago. "But you two…"

Marcus shook his head. "Nah, bro. I'm good."

"Me, too." Malcolm dated when it suited him and planned to remain a bachelor for life. He'd been down the road of heartbreak and would not do it again.

Once the head coach entered, the talk died down to a murmur as everyone slid into the leather theater-style seats.

"I want to thank you all for taking time out of your busy schedules to come in." His statement was met with laughter. He followed up with some general announcements, and then said, "We want to take a moment to honor Joe Marshall. He's been with the organization for twenty-five years and we're sad to see him retire, but he'll always be family. We wish you and Nancy all the best." Applause, whistles and shouts of approval sounded throughout the room.

Joe stood, nodded and waved. Joe's wife, Nancy, was battling breast cancer, and the special teams coach wanted to be there for her full-time.

"The next thing is we have a new dietitian on board. Please welcome Lauren Emerson."

Malcolm didn't hear the rest of the introduction. He struggled to draw in a breath, and his heart beat so loud in his ears it drowned out every other sound. He closed his eyes, hoping there was some mistake, but when he opened them again, she still stood at the front of the room.

Lauren moved to the center and shared some details about herself—background, previous employment and experience working with athletes.

Many of the younger players seemed to be spellbound by her presence. Malcolm heard Marcus whisper, "I think there's going to be more than a few guys camped outside her office."

Omar chuckled.

Malcolm said nothing. Her honey-brown face was as beautiful as he remembered, her smile still bright enough to light up a room and her curves sexy enough to stop traffic. Nothing had changed. Including his feelings. He'd never wanted to see her again.

Chapter 2

Lauren stared out at the room full of football players, her nerves a jumbled mess. Some sent flirtatious winks her way, while others' gazes held skepticism. But one pair of piercing light brown eyes bored through her. She didn't need a PhD to know that Malcolm wasn't happy about seeing her.

She ignored him for the moment and smiled. "Thank you for the welcome. I'm looking forward to working with all of you. I previously worked as a nutritionist and dietitian at a hospital in Phoenix and as a consultant with Arizona State's athletic department. I'll be working closely with you and the coaches. We'll schedule appointments with each of you to establish baselines, set goals and individual programs, as needed. Are there any questions?"

"Are you going to cook, too?" a player called out.

"No, but I'll be consulting with the staff chef."

Another player asked, "Are you married?"

Lauren laughed. "No." The question had nothing to do

with her credentials, but she figured the more they knew about her, hopefully, the more they'd come to trust her. She was under no illusions that the job would be easy, but she planned to be the best nutritionist the team had ever had. Lauren answered a few more questions then stood to the side as the general manager spoke. She surveyed the large meeting room that looked more like a movie theater, with its leather seats and a huge video screen that covered the front wall. The owners had spared no expense.

Her gaze shifted to Malcolm, who sat off to one side. His expression hadn't changed—it held about as much warmth as a blizzard. She discreetly studied the man she had intended to marry. The handsome face that had haunted her dreams so many nights had matured into one that she was sure had women drooling wherever he went and gave new meaning to *good-looking*. His athletic body looked even more toned, and the muscles of his chest and upper arms bunched with every movement. An image of her running her hands over his smooth, hard frame rose unbidden in her mind. She quickly dismissed it. With the way he kept frowning her way, she would be lucky if he even said hello, let alone came in for a scheduled appointment. The general manager's voice filtered through her thoughts.

"Before we end, I'd like to congratulate Malcolm Gray on being named one of the city's humanitarians of the year. He and his brothers and sisters will be honored for their work with the homeless community." Deafening applause broke out. Once it faded, he gave the date, time and place of the gala. "I'd like as many of us as possible to show our support." The meeting ended shortly after.

Lauren had no idea Malcolm's family held such prominent roles in the community. She turned and was immediately surrounded by several football players, who introduced themselves and cited all the reasons why they should have the first appointment. Though the big men towered over her like mountains, she caught a glimpse of Malcolm leaving out of a side door. Their eyes locked briefly, his so cold she shivered. Then he pivoted and strode out of the room without a backward glance.

She refocused her attention on the men in front of her and assured them she would be meeting with all of them as soon as she set up her schedule. Finally, they dispersed, except for one. He had to be at least six eight, and by his size, she guessed he might be a linebacker. He had dark skin and equally dark eyes.

He gave her a shy smile. "Ms. Emerson, I'm Darren Butler." He stuck out his hand.

His large hand engulfed her small one. "It's nice to meet you."

"Um… I know you're still working on your schedule, but if possible, can you give me one of your earliest appointments?"

The sincerity in his eyes tugged at Lauren. "Is there something specific you want to discuss?"

Darren glanced around, seemingly uncomfortable. "Yeah, but not here."

"I'll probably start having meetings by the end of the week. Can it wait until then?"

He nodded.

"I'll make sure to put you at the top of my list."

Relief flooded his face. "Thank you. I'll see you then." He inclined his head and made his way to the exit.

She hoped it wasn't anything serious, healthwise, and made a mental note to schedule Darren as one of her first appointments.

"You handled yourself well, Ms. Emerson."

Lauren turned at the sound of the GM's voice. "Thank you, Mr. Green."

"Have you had a chance to see your office?"

"Not yet." It had taken her a minute to find her way around the massive facility when she arrived earlier. By the time she'd somewhat figured out the layout, the meeting had been ready to start.

He smiled. "Then come on. Let me show you your new digs."

She returned his smile. They walked down a series of hallways, their footsteps echoing on the highly polished marble floors. He pointed out the locker room, weight room, training room, hot and cold spas, a few other meeting rooms, and a door that led to the practice field.

Mr. Green stopped at the dining hall. "Training camp doesn't start until next month, but the chef will be here later this week to meet with you. Nigel is a great guy to work with."

"I'm looking forward to working with him." She really wanted to ask what had happened to the previous nutritionist, since these positions weren't readily available, but kept the question to herself. Lauren surveyed the room. It was far from the cafeteria-style area with long tables and hard, narrow benches she had envisioned. It resembled an upscale restaurant—dark wood tables for four and six with matching cushioned chairs and half a dozen buffet stations.

They continued the tour until he stopped and opened a door. "Wow," she said softly when he gestured her into a spacious office easily three times the size of the one she'd had at the hospital. She walked across the plush carpeting to a huge mahogany desk on one side of the room that had an oversize chair tucked neatly behind it. Behind her, a half wall of windows overlooked a beautiful grassy area and walking trail. A small conference table took up space on the opposite side of the room.

"There should be information on all the players from last year in that file cabinet, and I'm sure you'll find some on the computer, as well."

Lauren glanced over to where he gestured.

"But, this is your show now, so you can set up a system that works best for you. It may take a few weeks for the players to get on board." He smiled. "Or maybe not, judging from the way they cornered you earlier."

She felt her cheeks warm.

"I'll leave you to settle in. If you need anything, let my assistant know."

"Thank you, I will."

Mr. Green gave her one last smile and departed.

Alone, her thoughts went back to his previous comment. Lauren had never had that much male attention in her life, even from the last man she'd dated. That relationship had ended six months ago. Her ex had been all for them climbing the corporate ladder together—as long as he stayed a rung above hers. He hadn't been happy when her salary topped his by a thousand dollars a year, and their easygoing, idyllic romance turned agitated and contentious. In the end, she tossed his ring and assurances of forever back and walked away, much like she'd done with the promise ring Malcolm had given her. She thought she had loved Jeffrey, but the moment she'd locked eyes with Malcolm, every memory and emotion she'd kept buried sprang to life. She realized she wasn't over Malcolm. Not by a long shot.

As soon as Malcolm parked his motorcycle in the garage, his cell buzzed. Without looking, he knew he'd see Morgan's name on the display. His stripped off his riding gloves, dug into his pocket for the phone and smiled. "What's up, sis?" He pressed the button to lower the door and entered the house through the garage.

"That's what I want to know, so I'll be over in an hour." Morgan hung up.

He released a deep sigh. He and Morgan always had that twin thing where they could sense when the other was bothered or upset. Based on his morning, he suspected she'd felt his emotional turmoil. He'd never expected to see Lauren again, especially since she moved to Arizona years ago for what she'd called a "better opportunity." Now he would be forced to see her damn near every day. To make matters worse, she looked even better than he remembered. As he'd noted during the meeting, the beautiful girl he had been in love with had grown into an even more beautiful woman. The curves he used to enjoy caressing were fuller and…

Malcolm cursed under his breath and ran a hand over his head. He stilled, remembering that he'd cut his hair a week ago, replacing the locs he had sported for over a decade with a scalp-hugging style that would take time to get used to. He climbed the stairs, took the short hallway to his bedroom, dropped his duffel on a bench at the foot of his bed and stepped out onto the balcony overlooking his large backyard. The June temperatures had warmed, and in anticipation of the annual barbecue he held for his teammates before the new season started, he had pulled out the deck and lawn furniture. He would need to cut the grass, but otherwise, the yard was ready for entertaining.

His thoughts shifted back to Lauren. He had to figure out a way to get out of any consultation with her. Malcolm's diet was just fine and his weight perfect, so he had no real need to see her. And that's what he would tell her. He glanced down at his watch. Knowing that his sister would be arriving soon and that she'd most likely want to eat, he headed down to the kitchen to prepare a late lunch.

Morgan rang his doorbell just as he removed the chicken breasts from the stove-top grill. He placed them on a plate and went to let her in.

"Hey," Morgan said. "Something smells good."

Malcolm chuckled and kissed her temple. "Come on in. I knew you'd want to eat."

She followed him to the kitchen and took a seat at the table. "Hey, you know I've never liked cooking. Nothing has changed. Lucky for me, my wonderful husband is an ace in the kitchen, and so is my favorite brother." She gave him a bright smile.

"So I'm your favorite, huh?" They'd been joined at the

hip since birth and there wasn't anything he wouldn't do for her. She was his baby sister by five minutes, and he took his charge as big brother seriously. It had been hard relinquishing the reins to her husband, even if Omar was his friend and teammate. He pulled out a bowl of mixed greens, sliced the chicken into bite-size pieces and added them. "How've you been feeling?"

Morgan ran a gentle hand over her rounded belly. "Pretty good. The only thing is whenever I sit for more than five minutes, this kid starts moving around so much, I swear there's a full-fledged game of tackle football going on."

"Well, you only have two more months to go. Did you and Omar change your minds about finding out the baby's sex?" Malcolm placed the bowl on the table, along with plates, utensils and a smaller bowl of salad dressing.

"Nope. We're going to wait. Of course, Vonnie and Faith are trying to get me to change my mind, talking about they need to know what to shop for." Siobhan, whom they affectionately called Vonnie, was the oldest of the five siblings. She and her husband, Justin, had a daughter who'd just celebrated her first birthday.

He smiled, got two glasses of iced mint tea and brought them to the table. "Faith isn't expecting, is she?" Faith and their oldest brother, Brandon, were trying for a baby, and Malcolm hoped they had good news soon.

She shook her head as she filled her plate.

Their mother was beside herself with being a grand-mother and with all of her children getting married. The only problem was that her attention had now shifted solely to Malcolm, the only single one. But he wasn't biting. As he had told his family countless times, he planned to be a bachelor for life. He loved the freedom to come and go as he pleased, and the ability to decide when he wanted to date. No hassle, no fuss. He would gladly accept the role of uncle and spoil his nieces and nephews.

After reciting a short blessing, he and Morgan started in on the meal.

"What kind of dressing is this?" She sniffed. "Lemon what?"

"It's lemon basil. Something I ran across at a restaurant where I had dinner. This is my attempt to recreate it. I used light sour cream to cut some of the calories, fresh basil, lemon juice and a little salt and garlic pepper. What do you think?"

Morgan ate a bite, angled her head thoughtfully and groaned. "It's really good. And that's why I come over here to eat when Omar isn't home."

Malcolm shook his head. "Did he go over to the center?"

"Yes. Rashad is finally going to talk to one of the psychologists, but he said he'd only go if Omar went with him. He's gone to a few of the group sessions, but that's it." Omar and a group of organizers had opened a mental health center geared toward veterans two years ago. Omar's older brother, Rashad, suffered from PTSD, and Omar wanted a place for Rashad and others like him to seek treatment that didn't center wholly around medication.

"I'm glad. I know how much he's been hoping Rashad would go." They ate in silence for a few minutes.

"What's going on?"

He glanced up from his plate. "Nothing. Why?"

Morgan stared at him a long moment. "So you're okay with Lauren being the nutritionist? I assume it's the same Lauren responsible for breaking your heart in college."

Malcolm set the fork down and pushed the plate aside. He blew out a long breath. "Yeah, it's her." Just the mention of her name conjured up an image of her standing in the center of the room earlier.

"I still owe her for that, so I hope I don't run into her while I'm at the practice facility."

"Let it go, Morgan." When Morgan found out what happened, she had stormed over to Lauren's dorm room, and he'd had to carry Morgan out to keep her from kicking Lauren's butt. In their family, the rule had always been mess with one, mess with all. It was even truer for him and Morgan. "She doesn't matter. I've been over her a long time." At least he thought so. Malcolm had been in several relationships since their breakup and hadn't thought of her once after the sting had died down. But his reaction to Lauren today told him he still had some lingering feelings that he'd buried.

Morgan took a sip of her tea. "What are you going to do about having to consult with her?"

"Nothing. I eat clean eighty percent of the time, work out four or five times a week, sometimes more, and my weight is fine. I have no need to see her." Malcolm knew Lauren would be sending out emails to all the players to schedule the preseason consultation—the same routine every year—but he intended to send her the same information he had just mentioned to his sister, with the numbers, and ignore her for as long as possible. He had to stay far away from her. His sanity depended on it.

Chapter 3

Thursday morning, Lauren made it to the Cobras' training facility at seven thirty. After three days on the job, she considered it a major accomplishment that she went straight to her office without taking a wrong turn. She powered up her computer, checked her schedule and read through her emails. She had sent a message to all the players and had three scheduled for today, including one with linebacker Darren Butler. So far, a little over half had responded, but not Malcolm. Not that she expected him to. A knock sounded, and her head came up.

"Morning. May I come in?"

Though the man wore athletic pants and shirt, she didn't remember seeing his face on the roster. He stood close to six feet with a trim, toned body, military-short dark hair and deep brown eyes set in a handsome olive-toned face. "Certainly."

"I'm Nigel West, the chef."

Lauren smiled and stood to shake his hand. "It's a pleasure to meet you, Nigel. I'm Lauren."

"The pleasure is all mine."

"Please have a seat." She gestured to the small table and joined him there. "How long have you been the team chef?"

"Going on six years. For the most part, it's been a blast, but there have been a few hiccups along the way," Nigel added with a chuckle.

"Tell me a little about the meal setup. I want to see what you already have before making any changes."

"Sure." He leaned back in the chair and crossed his ankle over his knee. "There used to be a variety of approved snacks available at all times and a good amount of fruits and vegetables. But over the last year, let's just say things weren't as tight."

"There were fewer healthy options."

"You got it."

Lauren wondered if that was what had led to the former dietitian being let go.

As if reading her mind, Nigel said, "When a few players weighed in at fifteen or twenty pounds over what had been reported, it was bye-bye, Stan. To make matters worse, he had taken money from two players who'd bribed him to lie."

"Are they still on the team?" If they were, she needed to know up front. In no uncertain terms would she be party to any of those schemes.

"Nope. They were sent packing with Stan."

It must have been kept hush-hush, because she didn't recall reading anything about a scandal or seeing it mentioned on the sports news. "Well, you won't have to worry about any of that with me."

He smiled. "I believe we're going to work well together. Let's talk menus."

For the next forty-five minutes, Lauren shared her plans, including color-coding stations based on the category of food, having a fresh vegetable and fruit station at every meal, and going back to providing the healthy snack options. "During training camp and practices, did Stan ever have your team make recovery shakes for the players after they worked out?"

"I mentioned it to him a couple of times after talking with a friend of mine who works with another team, but…" Nigel shrugged.

"Okay. I'm thinking a smoothie station might be something to add." Lauren added it to her list. They talked awhile longer, and by the time he left, she felt more confident. Not that she couldn't do the job, but working with elite athletes whose very livelihoods depended on them being in peak performance condition could be intimidating initially. And with her being a woman, she also had to endure the flirting, but she knew that would die down soon enough.

Her first two clients were team veterans and had a good handle on their dietary needs. They would only require check-ins unless something changed. Her third client, a rookie offensive lineman, was a different story. As she'd seen with most college students, athletes included, their diets consisted mainly of high-fat and processed foods—pizza, burgers, sodas and an array of sugary desserts. Trying to teach him to eat differently would be a challenge, and she had already made an appointment to go grocery shopping with him. She made a mental note to talk to Mr. Green's assistant about holding a diet and nutrition session for the rookies.

She was still chuckling at the player's disgruntled expression as he shuffled out of her office. Her cell rang, and she smiled upon seeing Valencia's name on the display. "Hey, girl."

"Hey, yourself. How's LA?"

"So far, so good. For the first time, I didn't get lost coming to my office this morning. It's only taken me four days. That's progress."

Valencia laughed.

"It's not funny," Lauren said, fighting her own laughter. "This place is *huge* and could double as a maze."

"I can't wait to see it when I come down." There was a pause on the line. "Have you talked to Malcolm yet?"

She'd known that would be the first thing her friend asked after hello. "No, but I saw him on Monday when I was introduced to the team. There wasn't an opportunity for chatting—not like he'd say anything to me anyway." A vision of the hostile glare he'd sent her way surfaced in her mind, and she involuntarily shuddered.

"You never know. Like you said, it's been a long time and you've both moved on. Is he still fine as all get-out?"

She laughed. "He is. The only difference is that he cut his locs."

"Really? I used to think they made him look so sexy."

So did she, and she remembered holding on to them as he thrust… Lauren jerked upright in her chair and shook the vision off. "Hey, girl, can I call you when I get home? I need to get ready for my next appointment."

"I should be home around seven, so any time after that is fine. Later, girlfriend."

Lauren disconnected and rubbed her temples. "What have I gotten myself into?" she muttered.

"Ms. Emerson?"

Her head snapped up, and she rose swiftly from her chair. "Come in, Darren. And call me Lauren." They took seats at the conference table and she turned the page on her notepad. "You mentioned needing to talk to me about something." She had read that the young man was in his third year as a defensive lineman.

Darren expelled a long breath. "Yeah. I lost my starting position because I'm twenty pounds overweight. Coach said if I didn't lose the weight by the time the season starts, I'd be benched." He looked at Lauren with sad eyes. "Can you help me?"

"Absolutely. But you'll have to commit to following the program."

"I'll do anything you ask," he said emotionally. "I worked hard to get that position, and I don't want to lose it." He threw up his hands. "And my girlfriend told me yesterday that she wasn't going to accept my marriage proposal unless I did something. Said she wasn't going to marry somebody just to become a widow when I die early."

Lauren didn't know how to respond to such a blunt statement. "Obviously, she cares a lot about you and your health," she said carefully. "And I'll be happy to help you. Training camp starts in a little over three weeks." She wrote down some notes.

"Right."

"Then we have work to do." For the next hour, they went over his current eating habits and the changes he needed to make. He grumbled and whined like a big kid at times, but in the end accepted her plan. "I want you to check in with me at least once a week."

Darren nodded. "Thanks, Lauren." He rose to his feet. "I'll see you next week."

"Call me if you have any questions."

"Okay." He left and closed the door softly behind him.

Lauren smiled as she shut down her computer and packed up to leave. All in all, it had been a good day. She slung her purse on her shoulder and made sure she had everything. Satisfied, she opened the door and hit a warm mass. She gasped sharply.

Mr. Green's blue eyes widened and he grinned sheepishly, his face turning a deep shade of red. "Sorry." He lifted a hand to steady her.

"No problem," she said, willing her heart rate back to normal.

"I just wanted to give you your invitation to the awards banquet I mentioned at the team meeting on Monday. It'll give you a chance to meet more of the management team and the owner."

His request sent her heart rate right back through the roof. She hadn't planned to attend the event. He stared at her expectantly, and she took the invitation from his out-stretched hand. "Thanks, I'll be there."

"Wonderful. Have a good evening."

"You do the same." It was bad enough having to see Malcolm. She wasn't looking forward to being in the same room with the rest of siblings, especially Morgan. After her breakup with Malcolm, the woman had wanted to rip Lauren's head off, and Lauren didn't think time would have changed Morgan's stance. *So much for having a good evening.*

Malcolm had avoided Lauren for over a week. He'd ig-nored the first two messages and then responded to her lat-est email yesterday informing her that he wouldn't need her services. Now, as he sat waiting for his brother, he read a message from the running back coach indicating an ap-pointment had been set up for Malcolm with Lauren this afternoon. This wasn't how he wanted to start his week.

"What's up, little brother?" Khalil rounded his desk, dropped a folder on top and sat. "You just returned from a three-week vacation in Brazil a little over a week ago, training camp doesn't start for another couple of weeks and, while everyone else is working on a Monday, you're off. I can't imagine one reason why you have that frown on your face."

"I was thinking about retiring at the end of the season, instead of having my agent ask for two more years."

"Is that right?" He studied Malcolm, no doubt reading him like he did everybody else in the family. Khalil had lost his hearing last year in an explosion and had had a rough time adjusting. Thankfully, he had regained his hearing fully in one ear, but even after surgery, he still had to wear a hearing aid in the other. At third oldest, Khalil tended to be the most easygoing and perceptive of the bunch, and Malcolm was glad to see him back to his old self…just not at this moment.

"You know a running back's lifespan is pretty short with all the punishment our bodies take. I'm just thinking it might be better to get out while I'm still healthy. Besides, with the second gym doing so well, it would be a good time to capitalize on the success."

Khalil leaned forward and clasped his hands together on the desk. "That was a great spiel. Now, are you ready to tell me the real reason you're in my office with this nonsense?"

Malcolm muttered a curse. He'd known his brother would see right through him. He hesitated a beat. "Lauren."

Khalil's eyes widened and he slowly sat up straight. "Your old girlfriend from college?"

"Yeah. Her."

Khalil frowned. "I'm not following. What does she have to do with your decision to retire early?"

"She's been hired as the team's new dietitian."

There was silence for a full minute before Khalil burst out laughing. "I can't believe it. I mean, the odds of that happening are, like, what…one in a million? Wow."

"Right. Wow. Not funny."

"I take it this is the first time you've talked to her or seen her in the eight years since the breakup." When Malcolm nodded, he asked, "While it's a shock, it shouldn't be a problem. You've moved on and I assume she's done the same, so…"

Of course he'd moved on. Malcolm had an active dating life and enjoyed women on his terms. Besides, Lauren hadn't exactly given him a choice about *moving on* after she'd accused him of seeing another girl on campus and broken things off without bothering to listen to his explanation. He felt nothing for her now. *That's not what your body said the other day.* Malcolm immediately dismissed the mocking voice in his head as not knowing what the hell it was talking about.

"Or maybe not. Look, Malcolm, you have a job to do. I've never seen you let anything, much less a woman, interfere with that job. You're both professional enough to deal with whatever issues you have."

He sighed wearily. "I know. I just didn't expect to see her, that's all. I'm fine."

Khalil checked his watch. "I have a client in ten minutes, but if you want to talk more, you can come by the house later."

A smile curled Malcolm's lips. "Lexia won't mind?"

At the mention of his wife's name, Khalil's face lit up. The two had gotten married nine months ago. "Nah. She's gotten used to all the impromptu visits and phone calls at all hours of the night." The siblings were all close, and it wasn't unusual for one to show up at another's home unannounced. However, now that all but Malcolm were married, the visits occurred less often.

He stood. "I'll see." Lately, he had begun to feel like the odd man out, especially every time his mother tried to tell him he would be happier if he found a nice young lady and settled down. Except he didn't see any reason to settle down at the moment, not when he enjoyed his single life. He had plenty of time to think about marriage and kids.

Khalil came to where Malcolm stood, and the two shared a one-arm hug. "See you later."

Malcolm took the stairs down to the main level and pushed through the doors leading to the parking lot. In his car moments later, he toyed with going home but decided to go directly to the facility. "Might as well get it over with," he muttered and started the car.

When he arrived forty minutes later, he sat in his car contemplating how he wanted to handle this first encounter. A riot of emotions swirled in his gut, most of them not good—anger, irritation and, somewhere deep down, a hint of desire. Finally, he got out and entered the building. He stopped to talk to a couple of the staff members then continued toward the offices. The closer he got, the harder his heart pounded.

Malcolm heard Lauren's laughter before he saw her. The same laughter he used to love.

"Thanks for your help," he heard her say. A moment later, she rounded the corner. "Oh, Malcolm. Hey."

He mumbled something he thought passed for a greeting.

They stood in awkward silence for several tense seconds before she said, "Um… I was just making…copies… We can talk in my office."

He gestured her forward but didn't comment. They stopped halfway down the hall at her door, and he followed her in. She had a pretty nice setup—spacious, expensive furniture, great view. Malcolm sat at the conference table and waited. As she walked past, he was treated to a view of her shapely backside in a pair of navy slacks that clung enticingly to her curves. The familiar scent of the soft citrusy fragrance she always wore wafted across his nose, and he closed his eyes briefly to block out the unwanted memories.

"Are you okay?"

Malcolm opened his eyes and met her concerned gaze. "Fine," he said tersely.

Lauren regarded him thoughtfully. "It's good to see you, Malcolm. I'm happy you've been able to live your dream."

"Thanks." Too bad he couldn't say the same about her. "Let's get this over with."

Lauren sighed softly. "Malcolm, I—" She squared her shoulders and opened a file folder. "They've already done the DEXA scan, and your bone, muscle and fat percentages are all excellent. For your diet—"

"I already emailed you that information, so we don't need to repeat it. My goals are to maintain where I am.

Simple. This is my eighth season, so it's not as if I don't know the drill." Malcolm didn't know how much longer he would be able to sit in this confined space with Lauren. He was torn between wanting to lash out at her for what she'd put him through all those years ago and kissing her senseless. He prided himself on having a good amount of control, but felt it slipping as the minutes ticked off.

Her pen stilled, and she looked up from the pad where she had been writing notes. "You did." She rose and retrieved a sheet of paper from her desk. "Height, six one, and weight, two hundred fifteen pounds. Diet consists of fish, chicken, lean beef and a variety of vegetables and fruits." She tossed the paper aside. "Look, Malcolm, I know this is awkward for both of us."

"Awkward? Is that what this is?" Malcolm leaped to his feet, and she instinctively took a step back. "Awkward doesn't begin to define what this is. Why are you here?"

Lauren frowned and folded her arms. "I don't know what you mean."

"You could've taken a job anywhere. Why *here*?" he asked through clenched teeth. "I don't want you here."

She placed her hands on her hips and leaned up in his face, her dark brown eyes flashing with anger. "Because this is where I wanted to work. I was offered an opportunity few get, and taking it meant being closer to my family. What was I supposed to do, check with you first? News flash, Malcolm Gray, I don't need *your* permission for *my* job choice, and whether you like it or not, I plan to be here for a long time!"

Something within him snapped and before his action registered in his brain, he hauled her into his arms and crushed his mouth against hers in a hungry and demanding kiss. Malcolm expected Lauren to push him away, slap him or make some kind of protest…anything, but she didn't. She kissed him back. And in the way that drove him crazy, like only she could.

"Malcolm," Lauren whispered.

Finally, sanity returned, and he jumped away from her as if he had been burned. *What the hell am I doing?* His breath came in short gasps, and his heart thumped erratically in his chest. His gaze was drawn to Lauren's lips, still moist from his kiss, and the rapidly beating pulse in her neck, which didn't help matters. He needed to leave *now*. Malcolm stepped around her, crossed the office in three strides and snatched open the door. He paused and turned back. "This changes nothing. I still don't want you here."

He strode out and didn't stop until he reached his car. He couldn't be around her for the next three years, especially not now. Not when he still wanted her.

Chapter 4

Several minutes later, Lauren still stood in the middle of her office, body pulsing, heart racing and mind reeling from Malcolm's kiss. Why hadn't she stopped him? And why had she kissed him back?

Memories of their relationship sprang up with such clarity she closed her eyes to block out the images. It didn't help. Lauren recalled every moment of the two years they had dated. But she couldn't let herself get caught up. She startled at the knock on her door. She glanced down at her watch. It was time for her next client. As she crossed the office to open the door, Lauren told herself she had a job to do, and that was the only thing she planned to focus on. She beckoned her next client in and, putting Malcolm out of her mind, sat and focused her attention where it needed to be—on her work.

Lauren didn't leave her office until after seven that evening and was back in the office at six Friday morning. She had her rookie training session at nine and wanted to make sure she had everything ready. At eight thirty, she met one of the office staff members in the room she'd be using, which happened to be a smaller version of the auditorium she had been in the first day. The woman gave Lauren instructions on how to work the video and audio equipment and departed. Lauren had just finished laying out the materials she wanted each player to take on his way out and making sure her presentation was on the correct page when the players started drifting in. At precisely nine, she began with an overview of nutrition and how it impacted performance.

"How many of you eat vegetables at least three times a day? No one? How about twice?" Lauren glanced around the room. Only two of the ten men in the room raised their hands. "Once?" Another three hands went up. She had her work cut out for her.

"I'm a defensive lineman and need these pounds. I can't tackle anybody if I'm all skinny and half-starved," a young man she hadn't met with called out.

"What's your name?"

"Brent Carroll."

"Well, Brent, you won't be able to tackle anyone if you're winded after five minutes or you can't move around fluidly and catch your opponent because your body is weighed down by all the useless high-fat calories you've consumed."

Low murmuring and deep chuckles sounded in the room.

"The goal here is to still meet your caloric needs, but with foods that will truly make you a beast on the field." A deafening roar went up, and she laughed. "Okay, so I guess that means you're ready to—" Lauren froze at the sight of Malcolm standing in the door. She promptly lost her train of thought. She turned to gather herself and, when she looked up, he was gone. Silently cursing herself for letting him rattle her, she turned her attention back to the waiting group and continued with her presentation. She heard a few grumbles and then gradually saw some nods. "Nigel and I have come up with some menus that incorporate more whole grains, vegetables and fresh fruits earlier in the day, along with the proteins to fuel your workouts. I'm going to add pre- and postworkout snacks, as well. For dinner, the emphasis will be on proteins and vegetables and lighter on the carbs, since you won't need them while you sleep. Any questions?" She acknowledged a blond-haired young man who looked to be barely out of high school.

"At first, I thought you were going to be putting us on a diet, but you're not, huh?"

Lauren smiled. "Well, not in the way you're thinking. No. The team and your fans are counting on you to get the job done on the field. I'm going to make sure you get it done off the field. And even when you're done playing football, you'll still be healthy." She took a few more questions, passed out the materials and scheduled each of those she hadn't seen for appointments. She had included sample meal plans and suggested shopping guidelines in the pamphlet, as well as her contact information should they have questions.

She had two clients to see after the session, including Omar Drummond, Malcolm's brother-in-law. Lauren found the gorgeous receiver far more pleasant than she expected, knowing how much Morgan disliked Lauren. Afterward, she spent the remainder of the day consulting with Nigel. She mentioned her earlier session with the rookies, to which he responded, "Hallelujah! Finally, someone who gets it."

At five thirty, she locked her desk and files, packed up her tote and slung it, along with her purse, on her shoulder and headed out to her car.

"Lauren, you have a minute?"

Lauren groaned inwardly and turned. "Sure, Mr. Green."

The general manager quickened his steps to reach her. "This will only take a moment. I know you're anxious to get out of here." He smiled. "I just wanted to hear how the rookie nutrition session went this morning."

"It went pretty well, actually." She shared what she'd told them, as well as their initial reluctance and the measure of acceptance. "I don't expect them to fall perfectly in line, but if I can change their eating habits now, they'll be better off in the long run. And so will the team."

"I agree. We did the right thing bringing you on board. Thanks, Lauren. I won't hold you. Enjoy your evening, and I'll see you tomorrow night."

"Tomorrow?"

"Yes. The award ceremony I mentioned last week. You'll be there, right?"

Great. "Oh, yes. I remember. I'll be there." Lauren couldn't very well tell her employer she couldn't attend because she wanted to avoid their star running back. "Have a nice evening." She continued out to the parking lot, tossed her bag onto the back seat of the car and slid in on the driver's side. She leaned against the headrest. Why hadn't she told him she'd be busy? "It can't be that bad," she rationalized. There would be a room full of people and, if her path crossed with Malcolm's, it would only be long enough for a polite nod. She started the engine. "I can do this. No problem."

When she got home, she called Valencia, hoping her friend could offer some advice about how Lauren should handle any further contact with Malcolm outside work. Part of her felt their relationship should be strictly business, but the parts of her that had responded to his kiss wanted a repeat performance. Valencia's cell went straight to voice mail, so Lauren would have to deal with her own emotions.

Her bravado held up all night and into the next morning. By Saturday afternoon, all of Lauren's boasting had been reduced to a mass of butterflies dancing in her belly. While she searched for a suitable dress in her closet, she wished she had begged off yesterday when she had the chance. Surely Mr. Green would have understood if she'd told him she couldn't make it. After all, she was still getting situated in her new place. She picked one dress after another but put them back. Finally, she settled on an off-the-shoulder black sheath dress that skimmed her curves, stopped just above the knee and had a modest side slit. Setting it aside, she went to shower.

Lauren dried off, wrapped the towel around her and hurried out of the bathroom to catch her ringing phone. "Hey, Valencia," she said, walking back to the bathroom.

"Hey. Sorry I missed your call last night. My cousin asked me to go to the movies with her at the last minute."

She activated the speakerphone and placed the cell on the bathroom counter. "No problem." She smoothed lotion on her arms and legs.

"What did you want? Is it about Malcolm?"

"Yeah. I never got around to telling you about what happened when he finally came in for his appointment. Well, he asked me why I took this job when I could've gone anywhere else."

"Seriously? Sounds like he's still angry."

Lauren recalled the confrontation. "Something like that. We kind of argued a little, but then…"

"But then *what*? Please tell me he didn't put his hands on you."

"No! Malcolm isn't that kind of man. He would *never* do anything remotely close to hitting a woman, no matter how angry he got." A memory of a girl in college who'd been upset by him shunning her unwanted attention surfaced in Lauren's mind. The crazy girl had gone so far as to shove Malcolm and throw water in his face. Malcolm had calmly told her, once again, that he wasn't interested and walked away. If anyone deserved his wrath, that girl had. Yet he'd done nothing. "He kissed me." Valencia was silent for so long, Lauren said, "Lyn, you still there?"

"Um…yeah. Okay, that was not what I expected you to say."

"I didn't expect it, either."

"And, so… I mean…what happened after that? Did you throw him out of your office?"

"Worse. I kissed him back." She slipped into her underwear, picked up the phone and went back to the bedroom.

Valencia burst out laughing.

"Not funny." Lauren placed the phone on her nightstand, picked up the dress and stepped into it.

"Oh yes, girl, it is. How was it? As good as you remember?"

"Better," she admitted grudgingly. "But he told me as he left that the kiss didn't change anything. He still doesn't want me there."

Lyn snorted. "I hope you told him that's too bad."

"I didn't get a chance to tell him anything, because he walked out. Now tonight the GM is expecting me to attend an awards ceremony for Malcolm and his siblings. They're getting some humanitarian award for work with the homeless. I really don't want to go, but I've only been on the job two weeks."

"True. And when your boss asks you to be someplace, you go."

"Exactly." Lauren examined herself in the full-length mirror in the corner of the room. "I keep telling myself that I'll be in a room full of people and, even if our paths cross, it'll just be a polite hello and keep it moving."

"Lauren?"

"Huh?"

"I know you've dated since then and your relationship with Jeffrey was pretty serious, but are you truly over Malcolm? Could you honestly say you felt nothing when he kissed you?"

She dropped down on the side of the bed and blew out a long breath. How she wished she could lie and say she'd felt nothing. That the kiss didn't make a blip on her heart meter. But it would be a lie. He'd had her heart beating at a pace that could be considered dangerous and sensations flowing through her body that should be outlawed. "No, I can't," she mumbled. "I told myself I was over Malcolm, and I am."

"Are you sure, sweetie?" Valencia asked. "What you and Malcolm shared was pretty deep. And it's hard to forget the first man you truly loved. Hell, if my first love showed up and kissed me, I'd probably succumb right then and there."

Lauren stuck her feet into a pair of black sandals with four-inch heels, fastened the ankle straps and chuckled. "You are crazy."

"Did you or did you not just tell me you kissed the man back? I rest my case," she added with a laugh before Lauren could respond.

"Shut up."

"Anyway, what are you going to do?"

"My job. It'll be easier for both of us."

"And if he wants more?"

"He doesn't."

"So you say."

"The man told me he didn't want me working there, so if that's not a clear sign that he doesn't want anything to do with me, I don't know what is." Hearing herself say the words, she knew this would be the best way, no matter how well Malcolm kissed. "I need to finish getting ready. Thanks for listening to my rant."

"Hey, you've done the same for me countless times. Let me know how it goes."

"I will." They talked a moment longer, then Lauren hung up. She applied light makeup, took one last glance in the mirror and, satisfied, left.

The gala was in full swing when Lauren arrived at the popular chain hotel. The grand ballroom was elegantly decorated, large chandeliers hung from the ceiling and a rose brocade pattern adorned the walls. She spotted several players, the GM and, on the far side of the room, Malcolm and one of his brothers. She couldn't remember which one.

"You made it."

Lauren turned at the sound of Mr. Green's greeting.

"Hi, Mr. Green."

He escorted her over to a small knot of people and introduced her to his wife, the team owner and his wife, and two more of the front office staff. "I was telling Mr. Lawler how much you've accomplished with the players in two short weeks."

The team owner, Mr. Lawler, nodded in agreement. "I'm impressed, Ms. Emerson, and I'm looking forward to having healthier players this year."

She smiled. "Thank you, Mr. Green and Mr. Lawler. I appreciate your confidence."

Soon they took their seats for dinner and the awards portion of the program. Lauren listened as Malcolm and his brothers gave short speeches. However, it was the one given by a man she didn't know—Cameron Hughes—that pulled at her emotional strings. He spoke of losing his wife and children in an accident and, unable to bear the pain, ending up homeless. But he also expressed gratefulness to his wife's best friend, who happened to be Khalil's wife, for not giving up on him.

Afterward, the music started and couples took to the floor, including Mr. Lawler and his wife. Lauren stood, intending to use this opportunity to go to the bathroom.

Mr. Green stood and helped her with her chair and waved at someone. "I know you're still meeting with players, but have you had a chance to meet Malcolm Gray yet?"

The hairs stood up on the back of her neck. Before she could respond, she felt the heat and, without turning around, knew it was Malcolm.

"Congratulations, Malcolm," Mr. Green said, shaking

Malcolm's hand. "Have you met Lauren Emerson? She's going to be a great asset to the team."

Malcolm stared down into Lauren's eyes. "Thanks, and yes, we've met. Hello, Lauren."

That's one way to describe it. "Hi, Malcolm." She had only seen photos of him wearing a tuxedo, and those pictures hadn't come close to capturing the raw magnetism he exuded standing next to her. She couldn't decide whether she liked him better with his locs or the close-cropped look he now sported.

"Well, my wife is going to have my head if we don't get at least one dance in, so I'll see you two later. Malcolm, can you make sure Lauren gets acquainted with everyone?"

Lauren's eyes widened. "Oh, I'll be fine. I'm sure Malcolm has some other people to see." She looked to Malcolm, expecting him to agree. To her amazement, he extended his arm.

"Shall we?"

With Mr. Green and his wife staring at her with huge smiles, she couldn't very well say what she wanted. Instead, she took his arm and let him lead her out to the dance floor. She regretted it the moment he wrapped his arm around her. Malcolm kept a respectable distance, but it didn't matter. His closeness caused an involuntary shiver to pass through her. And why did he have to smell so good? The fragrance had a perfect balance of citrus and earth that was as comforting as it was sensual. How was she going to make it through the next five minutes?

Malcolm must have sensed her nervousness. "Relax, Lauren. We've danced closer than this, so what's the problem?"

Lauren didn't need any reminders of how close they'd been in the past. "I'm fine," she mumbled.

A minute went by and Malcolm said, "Smile. You don't want everyone to think you're not enjoying my company."

She glared up at him. "You're enjoying this, aren't you?"

He grinned. "I'm holding a beautiful woman in my arms. What's not to enjoy?"

Mr. Green and his wife smiled Lauren's way, and she smiled back. As soon as they turned away, she dropped her smile. "I can't play these games with you, Malcolm," she whispered harshly.

"This is no game." Their eyes locked for a lengthy moment, then he pulled her closer and kept up the slow sway.

Lauren fell silent and tried to maintain her composure. The softness she saw reflected in his eyes gave her pause, given that it had only been a few days since their confrontation. She figured he was just being polite because they were in a room full of people, but deep inside, a small piece of her wondered if it was something else. Common sense said to let it go, but she couldn't. "Why are you doing this?"

Malcolm's brows knit. "Doing what? I'm just dancing."

She let out an exasperated sigh. "You know what I mean. Five days ago you wanted me gone. Now, tonight, you're acting like you don't hate me…almost like you care or something."

"I don't hate you, Lauren. At least not anymore."

She gasped softly.

"I won't lie. For about six months afterward…let's just say you weren't at the top of my favorite-persons list." He shrugged. "Now…" He let the sentence hang.

"A lot of time has passed, and we're not the same. I've changed and so have you."

He didn't say anything for a moment. "That's true. But there are some things that are still the same."

The last notes of the song faded, and he led her off the dance floor. "What are you talking about?"

Malcolm stopped near her table. "Your kiss." He pivoted and walked off.

Lauren stood stunned and unconsciously brought her hand to her lips. Realizing what she'd done, she snatched it down. She turned and saw Morgan glaring at her from across the room and hoped to escape a confrontation. She didn't need one more thing tonight. After locating upper management and a few of the players and saying goodbye, she left the ballroom. If Lauren were lucky, she'd make it out of the hotel and to her car without any problems.

When she took the job, Lauren had known she would have to deal with Malcolm, but she hadn't counted on this.

Chapter 5

Monday afternoon, Malcolm tossed another pass to the rookie running back who'd just been signed. He'd been more than surprised when Christopher Long asked him to help with some drills and laughingly said he wanted to be ready when Malcolm retired. Many of the younger players were hesitant to ask for help from the veterans, so it pleased Malcolm that Chris felt comfortable enough to seek him out. If the twenty-two-year-old continued to display the skills Malcolm had seen today, he'd be more than ready.

"Bring it in, Chris." Chris jogged over to where Malcolm was placing cones on the field. Malcolm gestured for the ball. "Now we'll work on the three-step cut." The drill helped a player develop lateral movement and cutting speed, both of which were necessary for eluding tacklers. It also helped improve ball-handling skills. "Let me see what you've got."

Chris nodded, assumed the position and started the drill. After he finished, Malcolm said, "Not bad. A little repositioning will help with your agility and speed. Place your feet shoulder-width apart, bend your knees slightly and keep your toes pointed straight ahead." He demonstrated the technique in slow motion and at full speed, then had Chris repeat the motion. They started at ten yards and increased the distance by five yards until reaching twenty-five. After the last round, they crossed the field and went inside to the cafeteria. Nigel was seated at a table with some papers in front of him, but he glanced up at their approach.

"Hey, Nigel."

"Hey, Malcolm." He extended his hand to Chris. "I'm Nigel West, the chef."

"Christopher Long."

"Camp doesn't start until next week, so what are you two doing here?"

"I asked Malcolm to help me with a few drills," Chris said.

Nigel stood. "How about I make you two one of the recovery shakes Lauren is implementing? You can be the test subjects. Chris, if you haven't seen her yet, make sure you schedule an appointment."

"I meet with her on Wednesday."

"Good. Have a seat and I'll be right back with the shakes."

Chris sat at the nearest table. "Thanks."

Malcolm followed suit. The mention of Lauren's name conjured up memories of their dance on Saturday night and the way her soft curves had felt pressed against his body. Just the thought spiked his arousal. He had done a good job putting her out of his mind for the past two hours, knowing she would be at the facility, but now she was front and center again. He just hoped to leave without running into her. Visions of how she looked in that body-hugging black dress that had left her shoulders bare had played havoc with his mind all weekend. He wasn't supposed to want her.

Chris's voice pulled him out of his reverie.

"I want to thank you for working with me today, Malcolm. My boys thought I was crazy for asking. Said no veteran would groom a rookie to take his position."

He chuckled. "Most wouldn't. But I'm not worried about you taking my position. Two years from now, it'll be all yours."

Chris laughed. "What else do I need to know to make it on this team? I know I won't be starting and most likely won't play but a few downs all season, but I don't want to get cut."

Nigel returned with the drinks. "Let me know what you think."

Malcolm waited until Nigel went back over to his table and resumed whatever task he'd been doing before speaking. "The first thing is you can't miss practice and expect to make the squad or be part of the game plan. Everybody takes bumps and bruises, but you work through them." He took a sip of the drink and grudgingly admitted that it tasted good, something like the ones he made for himself.

"What if I get hurt?"

"If you're seriously injured, that's a different story. You've been playing long enough to know that your legs will get heavy and muscles will ache, but the coaching staff needs to be able to trust in your ability to find a way to push through the day and answer the call if need be."

"Got it. I plan to be ready." Chris lifted the drink. "This is really good. Is this the kind of stuff Lauren will make me drink all the time? And is she going to put me on a strict diet?"

"The shakes are good for muscle recovery after a workout, so I assume they'll be available after practices. As far as a diet, Lauren will give you the tools you need to play your best game. You just have to follow her plan." They finished their drinks and headed for the showers. Malcolm took a moment to tell Nigel he thought the shakes would be a good addition. Obviously, Lauren knew her stuff.

Afterward, Malcolm slid behind the wheel of his black Camaro, started the engine and cranked up the air. The temperature had reached the upper eighties, typical for July, but once practice started, it would feel at least ten degrees warmer. He backed out of the parking lot and started down the two-lane highway. The facility was located four miles outside Buena Park and there was nothing but open space and a few trees along that stretch of the road. Halfway to the city limit, he spotted a car parked on the side of the road. A woman stepped out with a phone to her ear. Lauren. As he got closer, he was treated to the sweet curve of her backside in the gray slacks. Malcolm could see irritation on her face. He pulled up behind her and got out. He leaned against her car and waited until she disconnected. "What happened?"

"When I left work a few minutes ago, nothing was wrong. All of a sudden, the stupid car started losing speed and all it would do when I stepped on the pedal was rev up, so I pulled over and called the emergency road service."

From what she said, Malcolm suspected it might be her transmission. "How long did they say you'd have to wait?"

"Two and a half *freaking* hours," she said, scrubbing a hand across her forehead. "I don't have time for this." Lauren paced back and forth and then threw up her hands. "I don't even know where to tell them to take it."

He straightened from the car, intercepted her when she passed him and placed his hands on her shoulders. "Relax. I know a good mechanic. I'll call the shop and have them tow your car there, okay? You can call and cancel yours."

She let out a frustrated breath. "Okay. Thanks."

He pulled out his cell, made the call and arranged to have her car picked up. "It'll be about an hour."

"That's much better. Now I don't have to wait as long in this heat."

"You won't be waiting at all, because I'm taking you home," Malcolm said without thinking.

"Um...you don't have to do that." Lauren waved him off. "The wait won't be that long."

"No matter what has happened between us, you know

I'd never leave you here alone, Lauren. And it's too hot to sit out here."

Lauren stared up at him, apparently considering his offer. Finally, she nodded.

"Why don't you grab your stuff and lock up."

She reached into the back seat and took out a purse and large tote, closed the door, and locked it by remote.

At his car, helped her in then got in on the driver's side and pulled off.

"Still like muscle cars, huh?"

"Yep," he said with a smile. "And I have my motorcycle, too."

"I should've known you'd make good on it. That's all you used to talk about in col—"

The mention of college seemed to raise the tension and an uncomfortable silence ensued, but Malcolm didn't want to ruin the light mood. "I bought it after I got my first paycheck, just like I said." They shared a smile. He'd also promised to buy her an engagement ring with that check. One out of two wasn't bad. "So, where do you live?"

"Carson. I wanted to be close to my parents, but far enough to discourage surprise visits."

Malcolm laughed. "I totally understand. But my mother doesn't let that stop her. She doesn't think anything about the thirty to forty-five minutes it takes to get to any of our houses."

She turned in the seat to face him and groaned. "Are you serious? I hope my mother doesn't start doing that."

"Very serious." He told her stories of times when his mother had camped out at each of her children's homes and laughed as Lauren shared some of her own parent woes. He realized that he still enjoyed talking to her and wanted more time. "How about we have some dinner?" He took his eyes off the road briefly to gauge her reaction.

Lauren leaned back against the seat and stared out the window. "I don't know if that's a good idea, Malcolm," she said quietly.

She was probably right, but he ignored the warning bells in his head telling him to keep his distance. He didn't know why, but he wanted more time with her. "Think of it as an apology for my behavior last week."

"What are we doing, Malcolm?"

"We aren't doing anything. Just two people having dinner. Nothing more." Except maybe kissing again. The last time he had been angry, but it didn't change the fact that the passion still burned between them—or that she had kissed him back.

"All right. But what about my car?"

"When we get to the restaurant, I'll call and give him your number." Malcolm glanced at the clock on the dashboard, which read four forty-five. "The shop doesn't close until six thirty, and I doubt they'll close up before checking out your car and letting you know what's wrong. Since it's pretty early, I'm hoping we'll miss the dinner crowd. We can stop by afterward, if it'll make you feel better."

"It would. Thank you."

They rode the rest of the way in companionable silence, the only sounds coming from the hum of the air conditioner and the soft beat of the music playing.

"Ruth's Chris?" Lauren asked when he parked in the lot across the street from the restaurant.

"Yes. You don't like the food here?" Malcolm shut off the engine and regarded her thoughtfully. He probably should have asked where she wanted to eat, but the women he'd taken out in the past typically didn't care where he took them, only that he paid the bill.

"No, that's not it. Actually, I've never been to the restaurant."

"Good. I think you'll enjoy the food." He hopped out of the car, went around to her side and helped her out. She still wore a slight frown. "What?"

"I figured we were going somewhere less…elegant… and cheaper." She glanced down at herself.

He followed her gaze and took in the slacks and sleeveless blouse. "You look great, so stop worrying. We won't be put out," he added with a chuckle.

"Fine. But I'm paying for my own food."

Malcolm glared. "Nah, baby. I don't think so." Belatedly, he realized what he'd said. The endearment slipped out as if there hadn't been eight years of separation. He reached for her hand and escorted her over. Due to the early hour, they only had to wait ten minutes for a table. Fortunately, they were seated in a booth near the back.

"Tom will be taking care of you and your guest tonight, Mr. Gray." The hostess handed them menus. "Enjoy your meal."

"Thanks, Ms. Virginia."

Virginia smiled and departed.

"I take it you're a regular," Lauren said.

He shrugged. "I come here enough."

She shook her head and opened the menu. "Mmm-hmm."

Minutes later, Tom came to take their drink order, but both opted for water. With the season starting, Malcolm wanted to limit his intake of sugary and alcoholic drinks. He'd probably have a beer on Saturday at his barbecue, but that would be the limit.

Lauren closed her menu. "Malcolm?"

He lifted his head.

She seemed to struggle with her words. "I know it probably doesn't matter and is far too late, but I'm sorry for hurting you."

Malcolm slowly set the menu aside. For the past eight years, it hadn't mattered, but tonight, for some reason, hearing her apologize made him feel different. "It matters, Lauren, and I accept your apology. But I have to know why. Why didn't you give us a chance?"

"I don't know. I was young, insecure."

"Insecure?"

"Very much so. I was dating the school's star running

back, and more than one girl made sure I knew that I wouldn't be able to hold your attention for long."

His eyes widened in shock. "Lauren—"

She held up a hand. "Please let me finish. It was nothing you did or said. In fact, you made me believe that we could have forever." She took a deep breath. "One of my friends was dating an athlete at the time, as well, and the moment he had a shot at going pro, he walked away. He told her that he needed to be with someone who would run in the same circles."

Malcolm felt his anger rise. "That had nothing to do with us."

Lauren looked at him with sad eyes. "You're right. But seeing her misery and listening to her tell me over and over to get out before the same thing happened to me… I bought in."

He wanted to hold it over her head, but he couldn't. They'd both been twenty-one, and he didn't know a twenty-one-year-old who hadn't made a mistake, him included. And strangely, he understood her point. He'd seen a few of his teammates do exactly as she had described, and they'd ended up being linked to paternity suits, baby-mama drama or some other spectacle. Malcolm had never been a party to that scene, because his parents would have killed him— if his older siblings didn't do it first.

"If I could go back, I'd do things differently."

"I think that could be said for a lot of situations." Malcolm lifted his glass of water. "We can't go back, but we can start again. To the beginning of a new and mature friendship."

Lauren smiled and touched her glass to the side of his. "To new beginnings." She took a sip and set it down. "No matter what you think, Malcolm, I didn't come here to intrude on your life. But I appreciate your friendship."

Friendship. The word left a bitter taste in his mouth. After all they had shared, he didn't know if he could think of her as just a friend. Not when the first thing he'd wanted

to do when he saw her on the side of the road was take her
in his arms and reacquaint himself with the smell and taste
of her. Before he could delve further into areas where he
had no business, the server came with hot French bread
and butter and to take their orders. When he left, Malcolm
asked, "Why sports nutrition?"

"Actually, I have you to thank for that. During one of
our conversations about me going to grad school and having to write a thesis, I complained that I didn't want to do
the same subjects that everyone always did. You suggested
doing something related to correlating improved nutrition
to performance, and that's what I did. It worked so well
that I was offered a consultation position at the junior college where I conducted the study. It was only a few hours
a week, so I got a job at the hospital where I interned and
did that on the side."

That she had taken his suggestion filled Malcolm with
a weird sense of pride. "I'm really happy it worked out for
you, and I think you're going to do well with the team."

"That means a lot coming from you. Thank you."

Over dinner, he told her about his plans to join Khalil
in business and listened while she told him about wanting
to write a book on nutrition for athletes. As she spoke, he
couldn't help staring at her lips and remembering all the
ways they'd kissed—and all the places. He thought back
to the friendship toast earlier. Just friends? He didn't see it
lasting that way for long. Hell, he didn't see it lasting when
he took her home.

Lauren listened to the mechanic and felt a headache
coming on. "But the car is less than ten years old. How did
the transmission go out?" When she purchased the used
Maxima four years ago, she'd had it thoroughly checked
out and nothing came up.

He shrugged and handed her an estimate.

Her eyes widened at the cost. At this rate, she would

be better off purchasing a new one. "I'd like to check out some other options first before deciding whether to fix it. Can I call you late tomorrow morning?" She had too much to do to go looking for a new car. Fortunately, her first appointment wasn't until noon, but she needed a rental in the meantime so she could get to work tomorrow. She didn't want to impose on Malcolm any more than she already had, but outside of Uber or Lyft, she had no other way to get to the rental place. Her gaze caught Malcolm's. He gave her a sympathetic look.

"Sure thing." The man walked over to the other side of the long counter, retrieved a business card, wrote his name on it and handed it to her. "I'll just make a note that you'll call before we start any work on the car."

Lauren accepted the card. "Thanks." She followed Malcolm back to his car. "Thank you for everything."

Holding the door open, he asked, "You're welcome."

"I didn't mean to monopolize your entire evening. I know you're probably anxious to get home. Do you have to go far?" He'd been driving her all across town. Luckily, the repair shop had only been a short ten-minute drive from the restaurant.

A slow grin made its way across his handsome face. "Actually, I live about five minutes from here."

She faced him. "Oh, no. I can just call Uber or Lyft to take me home."

Malcolm's smile faded, and he shook his head. "Get in."

"Malcolm…" She trailed off when he folded his arms. He gestured with his head, and she sank into the leather seat.

Malcolm closed the door with a solid thud and then got in on his side. He leveled her with a look. "You do not need to spend money for that when I'm right here."

"But you'll be driving almost half an hour in the opposite direction, only to turn around and come right back here."

He ignored her and pulled onto the street. "So, are you thinking it might be cheaper to buy a new car?"

"I am. For now, though, I need to find a rental."

"I'll pick you up in the morning. Just tell me what time."

"I'm sure you have other things to do. I can just call—"

"Yeah, I know… Uber or Lyft. I'm taking you home now and I'm picking you up tomorrow. What's your address?"

Lauren refused to acknowledge how his possessiveness made her feel. Knowing she'd never win the argument, she rattled off her address. They discussed her options for the car and confirmed a pickup time for the morning. When he turned in to her complex, she directed him to a spot near her unit. "I appreciate your help, Malcolm. See you tomorrow at nine." She placed her hand on the doorknob.

Malcolm shook his head and chuckled.

She paused. "Now what?"

"You know I'm not letting you walk to the door alone."

She pointed to her unit less than fifty feet from where they sat. "Malcolm, I live right here. There's no reason for you to get out of the car. You can see me, and I'll wave when I get to the door."

"Stay there until I come around to your side." Without waiting for her response, he got out of the car and went to open her door. He extended his hand.

Lauren glanced at his hand, up at him and down again. She slapped her palm into his.

"You can glare at me all you want. I opened car doors and walked you to your dorm or your parents' house from day one, and that won't ever change."

She laughed and let him lead her to the condo. He had made it clear the first time they went out that he would treat her like a princess, and he always had. She used her key to let them in and turned to face him. "Safe and sound, okay?"

For a moment, he stood there staring at her with an intensity that made her heart race.

Malcolm lifted his hand and slowly caressed her cheek. "I know I said we'd work on being friends again, but…"

"Malcolm," she whispered. He lowered his head and covered her mouth in an all-consuming kiss. Unlike the kiss in her office, this one held no trace of anger, only passion. He slid an arm around her waist and pulled her against his hard body, making her senses spiral. She ran her hands up and down his back and heard him moan. Each stroke of his tongue conjured up flashes of their past relationship until the memories came back in a flood. Lauren felt herself losing control and broke off the kiss. "We shouldn't be doing this."

"Maybe not," he murmured, brushing his lips across hers once more. "I told myself that we needed to get along for the job, and friendship should be the only thing we should focus on." He held her gaze. "Am I wrong?"

She hesitated briefly. "No."

He smiled faintly. "Good. Lock up and I'll see you in the morning."

She watched his long strides cover the short distance to his car and then closed the door. This wasn't supposed to happen again. Sure, she had hoped they would declare a truce of sorts, but this? And what had he meant by *good*? This attraction seemed to be out of their control, but she couldn't see anything good coming from them starting up again.

Chapter 6

Wednesday morning, Lauren sat with Nigel discussing food placement and labeling the stations. She decided on a stoplight-type system to keep it simple—red for high-fat, high-calorie foods that should be very limited; yellow for foods that had nutritional value but still should be eaten in limited quantities; and green for fruits, vegetables, lean proteins and low-fat options. The goal would be to encourage players to eat from the green list most often. She had also decided to set up a smoothie bar with greens, fruits, yogurt, milks and protein powders, all labeled to assist players in understanding what each food provided for their bodies.

Nigel sat back in his chair and folded his arms. "Lauren, I know I've said it before, but you're a great fit for this team."

"Thanks." His words brought back what Malcolm had said over dinner two nights ago. Automatically, her mind shifted to the kiss they'd shared in the door of her condo. She hadn't been able to forget it or his words. When he picked her up yesterday, he'd placed a quick kiss on her lips, but nothing more. The parts of her that loved his kisses were disappointed, but the saner parts of her knew she should try to stop whatever was developing. Nigel's voice pulled her back into the conversation.

"And I know for a fact that those recovery shakes are going to be a huge hit."

Her brow lifted. "Oh? Practice hasn't started."

"No, but Malcolm Gray was here on Monday working with a rookie, so I made them the one with strawberries, pineapple, vanilla protein powder and orange juice."

So that was why Malcolm had been at the facility. Yet he hadn't mentioned anything about the smoothie over dinner. "They liked it?"

"Better than that. Malcolm mentioned it being similar to ones he made for himself. If the star running back is on board, it'll be easy to bring everyone else along."

"I'm glad to hear it. I hope they don't think I'm trying to be the food police. I don't expect them to eat healthy one hundred percent of the time, but if they do it close to eighty, I'll take it."

He laughed. "The food police? I think it'll be fine, but between me and you, a few of these players *need* someone to police them."

Lauren smiled. "I'll have the color-coded signs done by the end of the week, as well as the diagram for the station layout we discussed." She glanced down at her watch. "I need to get going." She gathered her notes and stood.

Nigel followed suit. "Showtime next week and we'll be ready. We can get together next Monday to go over the grocery list. Training camp starts on that Saturday, so I'll have my two assistants do the shopping on Thursday. I want to give us time just in case we overlook something."

She pulled up her calendar on her iPad. "I have some free time between eleven thirty and one—will that work?"

He picked up his phone and pushed a few buttons. "Let's make it twelve."

"Got it." She powered the device off and put it and a folder into her tote bag. "See you later." She made a quick stop at her office to pick up the shopping list for Terrell on her way out. She would be going shopping with the player to help him make better selections. Her cell rang as soon as she got to her rental. Lauren smiled upon seeing her father's name on the display.

"Hi, Daddy."

"Hey, baby. Sorry about not getting back to you last night. I didn't realize the phone was off until this morning. Did I catch you at a bad time?"

"No. I have an appointment in half an hour, but it won't take long to get there. I know you probably listened to my message, so do you think I should get the transmission fixed or buy a new car?"

"With the price they quoted, you'd be better off buying a new one. I checked around at a couple more repair shops, and the cost was about the same."

She opened the door, tossed the tote and her purse onto the back seat, and released a deep sigh. "I was afraid of that. I just paid that car off a few months ago, and I don't want to start up again."

"I checked into one of those pick-and-pull places, and you can get a couple thousand for the Maxima. Your mother and I can help you."

"I can't ask you guys to do that."

"I don't recall you asking at all. Now, when do you want to go looking?"

Lauren smiled and shook her head. She loved her daddy. "Saturday, if you're available."

"Got nothing to do but mow the yard."

Her father usually got up with the chickens and she figured he'd be done before ten. "If I came at eleven, would that give you enough time to finish?"

"Plenty."

"Thanks, Dad." They spoke a moment longer; she sent love to her mom and hung up. Lauren couldn't ask for better parents.

"Any news on your car?"

She gasped and spun around. "Malcolm. You scared me half to death. What are you doing here?" He had come up behind her without making a sound. She searched and saw his car parked several spaces over. She hadn't even heard him drive up.

"Sorry. I'm here for a meeting."

"Oh. My dad is going car shopping with me on Saturday. It's cheaper to buy a new one."

Malcolm nodded. "Are you done for today?"

"No. Going grocery shopping with one of your teammates."

He unleashed that sexy smile. "So, if I needed you to help me with food selection, you'd be available to go shopping with me?"

"*If* you needed help, yes. But you don't, so the point is moot." He moved close enough for her to feel the heat emanating from his muscular frame. She took a step, then remembered where they were and what she should not be doing. "I... I have to go."

He looked like he wanted to say something else, but he stepped back. "See you later."

Lauren quickly got into her car, started it and drove off. "You have a job to do," she muttered under her breath. "And that does *not* include dating a player three weeks after you start your new job. *But he's not just any player. He's the first man you fell in love with*, an annoying inner voice reminded her. Not that she needed any reminders. Her memory worked just fine. And that was the crux of her problem.

Malcolm stared after Lauren's car. After kissing her again, he'd told himself he needed to slow down and not get caught up. No reason to travel the same road, especially when he suspected the end result would be the same. When he had asked her to stay and work things out, she'd told him the move would be better for her career. With her just starting with the Cobras, he could see her choosing the job over their relationship once more.

"Hey, Malcolm."

He turned at the sound of Chris's voice. "What's up? You ready to work?"

"Let's do it."

They worked out for over two hours, repeating the previous drills and adding two additional ones that focused on agility and speed. If Chris kept the same work ethic and avoided injury, he would be more than ready to step into Malcolm's shoes when the time came. Now that the coaches used a Mobile Virtual Player during practice, injuries had decreased. The robotic dummies could mimic many football cuts and moves, and were used for tackling, chase drills and even as stand-ins for defensive players.

After showering, Malcolm planned to stop by the two transitional living facilities scheduled to open in two weeks. This would be the final piece of the project he, his siblings and Cameron started. The mobile grocery and shower had turned out to be so successful that they'd received donations to add two new buses equipped with showers and one more for fresh groceries. The buses traveled through areas with a high population of the homeless on a rotating basis. The hope was this small token would restore some dignity to the homeless population until they could get back on their feet.

His cell rang as soon as he got into the car. He smiled, started the engine and connected through the Bluetooth system. "Well, if it isn't the laziest engineer in Sacramento. What's up, cuzzo?"

Lorenzo Hunter's laughter came through the speaker. "Lazy, my ass. I'm not the one who only works six months out of the year." Lorenzo worked as a civil engineer at his family's construction company. "Since you're still slumming, you available for dinner tonight?"

"You're in my neighborhood?"

"Yep. Attending a conference. It should be over at four thirty."

"Cool. Come on over and I'll throw something on the grill. I'll text you the address."

"All right. Later."

Malcolm disconnected. He hadn't seen his cousin since Khalil's wedding last year, and he looked forward to catching up. Good thing he had driven his car instead of the motorcycle, because he needed to make a grocery run on his way home.

With some traffic, it took nearly an hour for him to get across town to the central Los Angeles neighborhood where the two side-by-side hotels that had been renovated as apartments stood waiting for their new occupants. They would house up to fifty men, women and families. It would have been more, but because the Grays had wanted to include families, some of the units needed to be larger.

The foreman turned, waved and started in Malcolm's direction. Malcolm met him halfway and extended his hand. "It's looking good, Mr. McIntyre." Though he knew the man to be in his fifties, he was in as good shape as Malcolm.

A smile creased his dark brown face. "They turned out better than I thought. Would you like to see inside?"

"I would." They passed landscapers, painters and other construction workers putting on finishing touches and entered a one-bedroom ground-floor apartment. The smell of fresh paint greeted Malcolm as he crossed the navy-carpeted floor. All would be furnished with appliances, furniture and basic supplies like towels, bed linens and toiletries; once the person or family moved in, groceries would be added to give them a head start. Malcolm took a few pictures to show his siblings. The place could easily fit two to three people. Next, Mr. McIntyre led Malcolm into one of the three-bedroom family units, where he took more pictures. "Your company did a great job."

"All we did was bring your vision to life, son. And I have to tell you, Cameron's suggestion of hiring some of the people who will be living here turned out to be a good one."

"I'm glad." Cameron had explained that allowing the residents to invest time and work in their new place would go a long way in restoring some of their self-respect and give them a deeper sense of pride, all while providing a wage. "I won't keep you. I just wanted to see the finished product."

"Will you be at the grand opening?" he asked, walking back out to Malcolm's car.

"Depends on the practice schedule."

The foreman's eyes lit up. The first time Malcolm had met Mr. McIntyre, the other man had quickly let it be known that he was an avid football fan with season tickets to the Cobras. "Oh, yeah. Training camp starts next weekend. I'll be waiting for that championship trophy again."

Malcolm grinned. "We'll do our best."

Someone called out to the foreman. "Let me get on back. I'll see you on the field." He shook Malcolm's hand once more and departed with a smile.

Malcolm chuckled as he drove off, scanning the buildings one last time and wishing they could have funded a few more.

He made it home twenty minutes before his doorbell rang. To his surprise, not only had Lorenzo come, but their cousin Cedric Hunter was with him. Their fathers, who were Malcolm's mother's twin brothers, owned Hunter Construction. "What's up? Zo, you didn't tell me this bum was tagging along." All three men laughed. After a round of one-arm hugs, Malcolm waved them in. "You both came for the conference?"

"Yeah," Cedric answered, taking a seat on the sofa in the family room.

Lorenzo sat on the opposite side of the sofa and leaned his head back. "Three days away from fourteen-hour days is heaven."

Malcolm dropped down in his favorite recliner. "You guys have a big project?" The company built everything from residential and commercial buildings to roads and bridges. Cedric, with his construction engineering degree, headed up the real estate division, while Lorenzo focused more on the larger-scale civil projects.

"That and the fact that Dad and Uncle Reuben are talking about retiring."

Cedric shook his head. "Ever since Uncle Nolan turned over the company to Brandon, that's all they've talked about."

Malcolm burst out laughing. "I thought you wanted to be in charge, Ced."

"I *am* in charge. I just don't know if I'm ready to be stuck in an office for eight hours a day. Hell, we're only thirty-three. Being co-CEOs will cut into my social life even more." Both Cedric and Lorenzo were one year younger than Brandon.

"Social life? You dating someone seriously?"

Cedric slanted him an amused glance. "Of course not. I like to keep my dating life fluid."

"Don't even look over here," Lorenzo said. "I need a break from women right now. And before you ask, she was into stuff that could have cost me my freedom."

Malcolm lifted a brow. "Illegal?"

"Yeah, man."

It sounded similar to what Khalil had recently shared had happened to him during his modeling days, except it had cost Khalil thirty-six hours in a Mexican prison.

"What about you, Malcolm? The women still trying to follow you when you're on the road?"

"No, thank goodness." His first year in the pros, Malcolm had been flattered by all the attention. But after seeing all the trouble some of his teammates had gotten into, he'd distanced himself from the madness and just focused on his game. Any woman he dated knew up front that if they shared any photos or personal information not already public knowledge, they would have trouble on their hands. He pushed to his feet. "I'm going to put the steaks on the grill. There's beer in the fridge if you want." In the kitchen, he preheated his stove-top grill.

Cedric followed Malcolm to the kitchen. "You know, you still didn't answer the question."

"What question?"

"The one about dating."

"I…no." He didn't know how to describe what was going on between him and Lauren. He couldn't call it dating.

Cedric burst out laughing. "Yo, Zo. Malcolm's going to be taking that marriage plunge with the rest of his siblings."

Lorenzo appeared in the kitchen. He and Cedric sat at the bar. "Really? Congrats."

Malcolm shot Cedric a glare. "Shut up, Cedric. I'm not dating anybody *or* getting married."

"I don't know. You should've seen the look on his face when he tried to answer, and then there was all the stuttering going on."

"Keep talking and you're going to find yourself starving tonight."

Still chuckling, Cedric held up his hands in mock surrender. "The only reason I'm backing off is because I'm hungry enough to eat two cows."

Lorenzo smiled. "So what's the deal, Malcolm?"

He paused in seasoning the steaks. "Lauren is back."

"From college?" they asked in unison.

"Yeah, from college." Malcolm shared the details surrounding her return, her work with the team and their first encounter—minus the kiss.

"Have you kissed her yet?"

He glanced at Lorenzo. "Why?"

"Never mind. You did. And you still want her, right?"

He didn't know what he wanted, so he remained silent. Instead, he placed the steaks on the grill. When he turned back, Lorenzo and Cedric were staring at him with wide grins. "Since you both think this is so funny, you can work for your supper." Malcolm pointed to the three potatoes and salad fixings resting on the other side of the counter.

Lorenzo shifted to face Cedric. "See, I told you we should've just gone to the restaurant in the hotel."

"I know, right? We could be chillin' instead of cooking."

"Whatever," Malcolm said, grabbing a bowl for the salad and shoving it at Cedric, who had come around the bar. They worked together until the meal was done, then carried their filled plates to the kitchen table. While his cousins drank beer, Malcolm opted for water. For the first few minutes, the only sounds were from forks scraping against plates.

Cedric lifted his beer in salute. "This is the best steak I've had in a while."

"Thanks."

"So, what are you going to do about Lauren?"

Malcolm paused in cutting his steak. "I have no idea."

"You'd better figure out pretty quick. The last thing you need is a woman crowding your head space like that, especially with the new season starting up."

He knew Cedric was right. He had to decide one way or another how to handle the rekindled attraction between him and Lauren. Common sense said to just let it go, but he wasn't sure if he could. Not wanting to dwell on it, he steered the conversation toward his cousins' families. They spent the remainder of the meal catching up on one another's families and talking sports. When it came time for them to leave, Malcolm offered to let them stay overnight, but they declined. With a promise to return for at least one of Malcolm's home games, the two men said goodbye.

As he cleaned up the remainder of the food and loaded

the dishwasher, his thoughts went back to Cedric's comment about Lauren. *No time like the present.* He checked the time—only seven thirty. He added detergent, started the machine and grabbed his keys.

Less than half an hour later, he knocked on Lauren's door.

Surprised filled her eyes when she saw him standing there. "Malcolm! What are you doing here? Is something wrong?"

"We need to talk."

Lauren moved aside for him to enter, closed the door and leaned against it. She folded her arms.

He had been so focused on what to say that he just noticed the skimpy tank and shorts she had on. The curves he'd felt the night they danced and when they'd kissed were on full display. Her folded arms emphasized the sweet swell of her breasts visible above the low-cut top. His gaze roamed lazily down her body to her toned legs and bare feet. His arousal was swift.

"You said you wanted to talk."

Malcolm took the two steps to where she stood, letting his body touch hers and wanting her to feel just what she was doing to him. He heard her breath hitch. "I don't know what to do about this dilemma. On the one hand, I should be keeping my distance. On the other…" He brushed his lips over hers. "I never want to let you go."

She closed her eyes briefly. "I didn't come here to complicate your life or mine, Malcolm. Only to do my job."

"Maybe not, but you're complicating it just the same. And as much as I want to deny it, there's still something between us." Lauren stared at him as if she didn't know what he meant. She opened her mouth and he added, "If you lie, lightning will strike you right now."

Lauren sighed. "We could ignore it."

Malcolm studied her. Less than three weeks ago, she'd blown into his life, forcing him to remember everything good about what they'd shared. And heaven help him, but he wanted to experience it again. "True, we could. But I don't want to, and your kiss says neither do you." Before she could refute him, he kissed her, slowly, provocatively, until all of her protests melted away. He banded his arms around her, lifted her off her feet and carried her into the living room. He lowered himself to the sofa and shifted her until she sat across his lap. "You were going to say?"

She punched him in the shoulder. "You know you're not playing fair."

"I'm not playing at all, baby." He captured her mouth again, slid his hand up her thigh and caressed her hip. Her hand moved across his chest, up and around his neck, sending heat straight to his groin and causing him to groan. He trailed kisses along her jaw and exposed throat, her faint citrus scent filling his nostrils and making him even harder.

"I...*oh*. I missed you, Malcolm," she whispered.

Malcolm went still. Her eyes snapped open, and he saw a look of panic, as if she hadn't meant to say it.

Lauren sat up and tried to leave his lap. "I—"

He tightened his hold. "I missed you, too, Lauren. More than you know." She relaxed. He had spent the last seven and a half years playing football, dating when it suited him and generally living life on his own terms. True, long-term commitments weren't on his radar, and he had been fine with that. And now she was back, invading his mind and his space. From the first, he had always found her easy to talk to—no pretense, no drama. She had been the first and only woman who respected his need for privacy. And ever since they'd had dinner, he'd realized he missed the easy rapport they always shared.

"So what does this mean?"

"I have no idea, but I do know that I want you. Maybe we can keep finding out, taking each day as it comes." Malcolm hoped it would be enough. Right now, he couldn't commit to more.

Chapter 7

"How did the barbecue go?" Khalil asked Malcolm Sunday afternoon, as they stood around the pool table at their parents' house talking with their brother and brothers-in-law.

"Fine. I didn't cook as much this year so I'd have less to clean up and put away. But I still have some grilled salmon left if you want it."

"Lexia and I will stop by on the way home tonight." He and Malcolm lived ten minutes from each other.

Malcolm grinned, knowing he'd say that. Khalil ate even healthier than Malcolm. He'd been a model for close to a decade before studying for his kinesiology and business degrees and opening up a fitness center. "Speaking of Lexia, when is her book signing?" Khalil's wife had written a cookbook geared toward college students.

"Two Saturdays from now. She's excited, but a little nervous with it being her first book. She's worried no one will show up and no one will buy the book." He lined up his shot and just missed the pocket.

"The way she cooks, I don't think she'll have any problems with people buying her book," Brandon said. "We'll all be there to support her."

Justin took his turn at the table and sank his shot. "And with this brood, she won't have to worry about the bookstore being empty."

They all laughed. All of Malcolm's siblings had gotten married in a space of less than four years, and if everyone's parents and extended family were in attendance, Justin's assessment would be correct. Only Malcolm and Omar would possibly miss it, due to the start of training camp.

"I haven't checked the practice schedule, so I don't know whether I'll be able to attend," Omar said.

Malcolm nodded in agreement. "Oh, Lorenzo and Cedric were here this week."

Brandon paused with a water bottle halfway to his lips. "Really? Why didn't you invite them over?"

"I did, but they had to get back to Sac. They said they'd be back during the season."

Morgan stuck her head in the door. "Dinner, guys."

Khalil and Justin replaced the pool sticks, and they all filed out and took seats at the large dining room table that his mother insisted she needed to accommodate the growing family. She was ecstatic about her granddaughter, Nyla, and the pending birth of Morgan and Omar's first child. Along with Nyla, Siobhan and Justin were going through the process of adopting a four-year-old boy named Christian. Though the little boy had spent time with Siobhan and Justin, today was his first time meeting the rest of the family. It hadn't taken him long to become comfortable and Malcolm had distinctively heard him call Malcolm's mother Grandma. In order to allow for the extra time, the social worker had agreed to pick him up from here later.

Once everyone had a seat, Malcolm's father blessed the

food, and conversation commenced as plates were filled. Malcolm watched Siobhan's relaxed features as she smiled and fed her daughter. For years, she had blamed herself for Malcolm getting hurt during one of his daredevil stunts after she had gone out with friends as a teen instead of staying home while their parents were out. Marriage and motherhood had mellowed her a great deal, and Malcolm couldn't have been happier.

Malcolm forked up some of the macaroni and cheese and stifled a groan. No one could hold a candle to his mama's version, and he'd be working out extra hard tomorrow because he planned to have another helping.

"How is Lauren working out with the team?"

He stared at Brandon. Somehow, he'd known he wouldn't be able to get through dinner without someone asking.

"Specifically, how are things working out between you two with her being there?"

Confused. Complicated. Unsettling. Pick one. Keeping his voice neutral, he said casually, "Fine. She's doing her job and I'm doing mine."

Khalil leaned back and studied Malcolm. "Is that right? Because you two looked *real* cozy on the dance floor last Saturday night."

"It was nothing."

Morgan pointed her fork Malcolm's way. "Whatever. Cozy or not, she'd better not hurt you again."

Malcolm lifted a brow and shook his head at his twin. "Morgan, I think I can handle my life just fine. Oh, I stopped by the transitional housing the other day, and it looks great," he said, changing the subject.

"I'm just so proud of you all," his father said. "Your mother and I will be at the grand opening. Thad said he'd be there as well." Thaddeus Whitcomb, whom they affectionately called Uncle Thad, was his father's best friend and business partner. Malcolm and his siblings had been shocked to find out Uncle Thad had a daughter, who he'd found after several years of searching. Malcolm chuckled inwardly remembering all the fireworks that sparked between Brandon and Faith when he found out she was that daughter and stood to inherit part of the company Brandon had thought he would be running solo. They were now happily married.

"How many families will they house again?" Justin asked.

"Up to fifty for each building."

"And that's one hundred less on the streets." His mother sighed. "I just wish the city would do more. It doesn't make sense to have all these vacant buildings sitting around when they can be put to good use."

Siobhan laughed. "Uh-oh, y'all got Mom started."

"Hey, she does have a point," Lexia said.

Faith held up her hand and high-fived Lexia. "Agreed."

Laughter flowed around the table, and they continued eating and conversing until plates were clean. Afterward, everyone shuffled to the family room and relaxed, too full to do anything else for the time being. However, an hour later, no one turned down the peach cobbler and homemade vanilla ice cream served for dessert.

Christian devoured his portion in a matter of minutes, then held his empty bowl out. "Grandma, can I have more ice cream?"

Malcolm's mother beamed. "Of course, baby." She set her bowl aside, stood and took his hand. "Come on and let's get you some."

Justin shook his head. "Two hours and he's got your mom wrapped around his finger."

Siobhan playfully elbowed him. "And he doesn't have you wrapped, too?"

Christian came back wearing a huge smile and sat on the floor next to Malcolm.

Malcolm ruffled his head. "You're going to have to do a lot of exercising to work off all this dessert, little man."

The boy just smiled around a huge spoonful of ice cream.

They were just finishing when the social worker arrived. No one wanted Christian to leave, especially Malcolm's mother and Siobhan. Christian's little sad face moved Malcolm in a way he hadn't anticipated. He had no idea how many more trial weekends were necessary, but he hoped not many, because Christian had captured all their hearts.

After several rounds of goodbyes, Christian ran over and wrapped his arms around Siobhan's waist. "Mama, *no*! I want to stay with you," he cried.

Malcolm heard Siobhan's sharp gasp and saw her fighting for control. His mother and Morgan looked stricken, as did Faith and Lexia.

Justin rushed over and gently scooped up Christian. "Malcolm, take Siobhan out of here!" He strode toward the door with the screaming little boy.

"No! Mama!"

Malcolm picked his sister up, carried her to one of the extra bedrooms and placed her on the bed.

"My baby, my baby. He's never called me Mama before." Siobhan jumped up from the bed and started toward the door, but Malcolm blocked her way. "Tell Justin he can't let her take him," Siobhan pleaded as she wept.

Seeing his sister, always the strong one, who never lost control, crying this way broke Malcolm's heart. "Everything's going to be okay, Vonnie. This is only temporary. Christian will be with you before you know it." Not knowing what else to say, he just held her. She was still crying when Justin came in a few minutes later. He kissed his sister on her forehead. "How's Christian?"

Justin's pain was reflected in his face. He shook his head. "He's never done this before. It nearly killed me to put him in that car. She said we'd probably be able to have him for good in two or three weeks. I hope so, because I can't go through this again." He gathered Siobhan in his arms and led her back to the bed. "Thanks, Malcolm."

Malcolm nodded and left quietly. He found everyone still subdued when he entered the family room. He, Brandon and Omar put away the food and loaded the dishwasher, then everyone said their goodbyes.

Hours later, long after Khalil and Lexia had come and gone, Malcolm sat on the balcony off his bedroom, unable to get the sound of Christian's screams out of his head. Back when they were dreaming, he and Lauren had talked about having children, but he hadn't thought about it since then. Tonight, however, those imaginings came back full force and, for the first time in eight years, he contemplated what it would be like to have children of his own. The realization startled him and he quickly shoved it aside. He needed to keep his focus on the upcoming season and not the crazy musings of two kids who had fancied themselves in love. He could handle that. He hoped.

Monday morning, Lauren had her hands full with the third day of training camp. Fortunately, she eased into the transition, somewhat, since only the twenty-seven rookies started for the first two days. But by Friday, the entire fifty-three-man lineup and an additional ten reserve players had descended on the facility. When she arrived at six thirty, she passed several players in the gym and in the various meeting areas.

"Man, by the time the season starts, I'd better be a lean, mean blocking machine, eating all this healthy stuff."

Lauren cut a look at Brent. He'd complained their entire session. She leaned over to see what he had on his breakfast plate.

"See, Lauren, a six-egg omelet with spinach, mushrooms and red peppers, salmon cakes, whole-wheat bagel, two bananas, yogurt, and milk."

She patted his arm. "Nice job. You'll be energized for

practice instead of moving like a slug." She wanted the line-man to keep the mass and protein levels higher because of the constant contact he'd have during games. For the play-ers who ran more, increased carbohydrates and good hy-dration were the key.

Brent laughed. "You're cool people, Lauren."

She couldn't help but smile. "Thanks. So are you." She went over to where Darren stood scooping eggs. He'd lost nine pounds already and needed to lose eleven more. Even so, he still needed a little over five thousand calories a day.

"Hey, Lauren. What else is on the list? I have the four scrambled eggs and I added the spinach and mushrooms to get in some veggies."

"Oatmeal, turkey sausage and a smoothie made with two scoops of protein powder, low-fat milk, peanut butter and a banana." She had one of the guys from Nigel's team make the smoothie. This was going better than she had hoped. Lauren turned and went still at the sight of Mal-colm making his way over to the buffet. He glanced her way, smiled faintly and picked up a plate. Moments later, she sensed him behind her.

"I like the signs." Malcolm filled his plate.

"Thanks." He reached for a bagel and his arm brushed hers, the contact sending heat spiraling through her.

"What made you decide to do this?"

"I thought it would be a good way to bring attention to what everyone is eating. When it's in your face, it's hard to miss."

He studied her. "Good point. It is hard to miss some-thing when it's right in your face."

The way he looked at her and the softness in his voice told her he meant something else altogether. "I...need to get going. Have a good practice." Without waiting for a reply, Lauren made a beeline for the kitchen area. Just seeing Malcolm conjured up visions of his mouth and hands on her last week. Standing next to him pretending that nothing was going on between them and that she barely knew him tested her in ways she couldn't begin to describe.

She shook herself and continued to make her rounds in the dining room, stopping to talk to players and answering any questions. However, she felt Malcolm's gaze whenever she passed him. She was relieved when the dining area emptied out.

"You did well in all this chaos," Nigel said, coming her way. "I couldn't believe how many players asked for the added veggies in their eggs or omelets. Then again, with someone so pretty asking, they'd probably eat a bowl of castor oil to please you."

Lauren made a face. "I hope not. Do you need me for anything else before lunch? If not, I'll be in my office."

"Nope. My guys can handle the smoothies or the players themselves, so we'll see you later."

She spent the next two hours updating player profiles and answering emails. Then, curious about the practice, she made her way outside, stood at the edge of the tunnel leading to the practice field and watched them run plays. She searched until she saw Malcolm at the far end of the field, marveling at his agility, speed and the way the muscles in his legs flexed with every movement. He was at the top of his game, and she couldn't imagine a time when he'd have to give up the game he loved.

Lauren took a quick peek at her watch and headed back. Practice would end in the next hour, and she wanted to make sure the staff laid out lunch to her satisfaction. She figured she wouldn't need to be too involved in the kitchen in a couple of weeks and could spend her time individually with the players and coaches. Today's lunch consisted of grilled chicken breasts, top sirloin steak, brown rice, sweet potatoes, a variety of green vegetables and salad and fruit bars.

After lunch ended, Lauren collapsed in her office chair and let out a long breath, but she had a smile on her face.

All in all, it had been a good day. The last meeting ended at four thirty and Nigel would be preparing dinner, but Lauren didn't feel she needed to stay around for that. *I'm loving this job.* She allowed herself a few minutes of quiet—being around over fifty giants could get pretty loud—then got to work.

She was so engrossed in the figures on her computer screen that she jumped at the sound of a knock on the partially opened door. "Come in."

"Hey."

"Hey, Malcolm. What are you doing here? Practice is over?" He had showered and changed into a pair of basketball shorts and fitted tee.

"It's almost six. What are *you* still doing here?"

"I guess I lost track of time." She stood and stretched. "You didn't answer my question."

Malcolm hesitated a beat. "I wanted to know if you had any plans tonight."

"Um…no, not really. Why?"

"I wanted you to come to my place so we can talk. I know you haven't had dinner. I can fix something."

Lauren's mind screamed, *don't do it!* Malcolm had readily admitted that he didn't want to let their attraction die down, but she continued to have reservations about starting up with him again. However, curiosity about where he lived got the best of her, and she agreed before fully considering the ramifications of her choice. "I should be ready to leave in about ten minutes. Um…" She didn't want them to walk out together, giving anyone reasons to speculate.

"I'll wait for you in the parking lot."

His expression told her he wasn't too fond of the idea, but she had to protect her reputation. "Thank you."

"See you in a few."

As soon as he was gone, Lauren dropped her head in her hands. "What am I doing?"

Chapter 8

Lauren discreetly scanned the parking lot as she walked to her car. A few players stood around talking, while others leaving passed her with a wave. She spotted Malcolm about ten spaces away getting into his car. Her phone rang as she opened the door, and she hurriedly got in and dug it out of her purse. Seeing Malcolm's name on the display, she glanced around again. "Hey."

"No one can tell who you're talking to on the phone, Lauren, so you can stop looking like you're about to do something wrong," Malcolm said with a laugh. "And before you say anything, there aren't any rules or policies against us dating."

"I'm not thinking about that," she lied. A guilty expression crossed her face. He had voiced her exact concerns. She knew about the no-fraternization policy between players and cheerleaders and had wondered if it extended to all staff.

"If you say so. Anyway, I'll meet you on the road."

"Okay." She disconnected, started the car and backed out. She noticed him waiting a few hundred feet ahead. When he saw her approach, he pulled off in front of her. During the entire drive, Lauren questioned her sanity. While there were no written rules, surely this would be frowned upon. "What are you thinking, agreeing to go to his house?" she muttered. Two miles onto the freeway, traffic slowed to a crawl. This was the one thing she didn't miss about home, and it seemed to have gotten worse over the years. It finally picked up several minutes later, and she began to have second thoughts. It would be really easy to keep going to her place. As if he read her mind, she caught his gaze in his rearview mirror, probably checking to see if she was still following. He'd said he wanted to talk, but he'd said the same thing when he showed up at her place last week. Somehow, his definition of *talking* differed from that of the rest of society. *Not that you minded*, an inner voice argued.

She drew in a deep, calming breath. He'd mentioned cooking. They'd talk over dinner and she would leave right after. There. A good, solid plan that didn't involve kisses. Now, if she could just follow through.

The traffic finally lightened up and they made the rest of the drive in fifteen minutes. Lauren expected Malcolm to live in a gated community. Instead he drove into an upscale neighborhood with large, stately homes. His was located in the center of a cul-de-sac that held only five houses. Malcolm stopped in the driveway, and one of the three garage doors lifted. He gestured for her to pull into the driveway behind him.

With daylight savings time, the sun hadn't yet set, and she had a clear view of his magnificent Mediterranean-style home—red tile roof, archways and tile walkway. Inside the garage, she could see his motorcycle and smiled.

Malcolm parked in the garage, got out and came toward her. "What are you smiling about?"

"The motorcycle."

He glimpsed over his shoulder. "We can take a ride if you want."

"That's okay." Lauren shouldn't have cared, but she wondered how many other women he had taken for a ride. *When I get my bike, you'll get the first ride.* The memory rose unbidden and shocked her. He had made the promise years ago, but she doubted he remembered.

"You sure? I have an extra helmet that I kept for Morgan until Omar bought her one of her own."

"Positive." He made it sound as if no other woman had used it, and she felt a measure of relief. *Get it together, girl!* "Your home is beautiful," she told him, needing to change the subject.

Malcolm smiled. "Thanks. Come on in and I'll give you a quick tour before dinner."

She followed him up the walk to the wooden double doors and waited for him to unlock it. He moved aside for her enter. She stopped inside the door with wide eyes and stared at the winding twin staircases that showcased an expansive second story. The highly polished wood floor in the short foyer led into a formal living room with expensive furniture and plush carpeting. A formal step-up dining area with the same wood flooring sat slightly behind the living room. He had a chef's kitchen—equipped with every modern appliance known to man—that opened into a breakfast nook and large family room. Each space flowed into the next and was separated by huge columns. "You must do a lot of entertaining."

He spun around. "Why would you say that?"

She waved her hand around. "The floor plan is so open, and it's the perfect kind of house for lots of gatherings. How long have you lived here?"

"Four years. And the only gatherings I have are the ones where my family comes over and the barbecue I host for a few of my teammates every year before the season starts. I don't like a lot of people in my space."

Lauren smiled. "I guess you haven't changed."

He met her smile with one of his own. "You know better than most how much I value my privacy. That won't ever change." He reached for her hand and started up one set of stairs.

"How many bedrooms do you have?"

"Five."

"Five?"

"My brothers and sisters and I usually hang out at each other's houses and stay overnight, so whoever stays has a place to sleep. But since they've all gotten married, we don't do it as much."

"You have a library, too." An open nook at the top of the stairs had been outfitted with two comfortable chairs, a small table and three filled bookshelves. They both enjoyed reading and it hadn't been uncommon for them to spend hours on the weekend reading together. He showed her three tastefully decorated guest bedrooms, each with en suite bathrooms. The master bedroom occupied the entire opposite side of the floor. Lauren shook her head. "I think you're taking this whole privacy thing a little far."

Malcolm laughed and shrugged. "Hey, I didn't build the house."

"But I bet it was the thing that sealed the deal for you."

He gestured her forward. "I plead the Fifth."

She rolled her eyes as she entered the room. "Mmm-hmm." Just like the rest of the house, he'd spared no expense. Dark, heavy furniture accentuated the space, but the big bed remained the focal point. A television had been mounted on the wall, a sophisticated sound system took up a portion of the far wall and a sitting room connected via an archway. He had a private deck, a bathroom with a spa tub and marble shower, both of which could easily fit two people, and an extensive walk-in closet. "This is beautiful, Malcolm. I thought you said you have five bedrooms."

"Thanks. And the other one is downstairs off the family room." He stood there a moment just looking at her.

"Something wrong?"

He closed the distance between them. "No. I just…"

"Why did you invite me here?"

He tilted her chin until their eyes met. "Because the first thing I wanted to do when I saw you today was kiss you."

She opened her mouth to protest, and he kissed the words right off her lips. He drew her closer, his tongue twirling with hers and sending waves of pleasure through her. He lifted her until she felt the hard ridge of his erection pressed against her center and she moaned.

Malcolm walked over to the nearest wall and held her in place. He gripped her buttocks and brushed kisses along the shell of her ear. "Why are you doing this to me? Do you feel how much I want you, baby?"

"I…" Her breath came in short gasps and she found it impossible to form words. But, truth be told, she wanted him, too.

His hand feathered up her torso to her breast. "I want to touch you and watch you come apart in my arms," he murmured.

He captured her mouth again, and the sensations were so staggering she was three-quarters of the way to orgasm already. A *kissgasm* was the only way she could describe it. "Malcolm."

He eased back, his breathing just as ragged as hers. "I know what you're going to say. Tell me you don't feel this and I'll stop."

Lauren stared into the eyes that had sucked her in the first day she saw him sitting in a biology class and that held her captive even now. "You know I do, but what about my job?" She wanted to call the words back as soon as they left her mouth when she saw the split second of pain that crossed his handsome face. "I'm not choosing my job over you, if that's what you're thinking."

Malcolm didn't respond immediately. Finally he said, "I know what you meant. What if we keep this between us until we can figure it out?"

"Okay." She kissed him softly, appreciating him seeing her point of view.

He gently lowered her to her feet. "Let's go get some dinner. I'm back on the clock now and can't be out too late."

"How are you breaking curfew if you're at home?" she asked as they descended the stairs.

"I have to follow you home."

"No, you don't."

"I'm not going to argue with you and I *am* following you home, so let it go."

"Fine."

Later, while eating, Lauren thought about their agreement, and it should have made her happy. But somewhere in the back of her mind, she was afraid they would end up just as they had eight years ago.

After following Lauren home, Malcolm stood beneath the warm stream flowing from his shower thinking about her and his agreement to a secret relationship. He admitted to himself that she had been right about where his thoughts had gone when she mentioned her job. A part of him still questioned whether she'd make the same choice and whether he would get the short end of the stick again. But he could no more stop his growing feelings than he could turn day to night. He finished his shower, made sure he'd turned on the alarm and slid beneath the cool, crisp sheets on his bed. The clock only read ten—early by most thirty-year-olds' standards—but football was his life, and his longevity depended on him doing the right things.

When he first started in the league, two of the veteran players had come to him and asked about his career aspirations. When Malcolm had voiced his desire to play for at least ten years, they immediately told him that meant eating right, cutting out all the partying and going to bed at eight thirty during the season. He'd laughed at the time, but within two months he began to see the wisdom of their advice. He'd never had a big problem when it came to eating, but he did occasionally hang out on the weekends and stay up late with some friends from college. Practices were much more grueling with no rest, so he'd known he had to make some changes or risk losing everything he had worked for since age eight.

Malcolm still went out, but he didn't drink alcohol and left early. And he started going to bed no later than ten. His game improved dramatically, and he'd kept the practice up until now. Several of the players who started their professional careers at the same time as Malcolm had washed out of the league in less than three years because their on-the-field performance had been negatively impacted by all of bad habits they'd adopted—partying and drinking, not eating properly, and consistently breaking curfew—landing them in trouble no team wanted to deal with. Although Cobras management didn't check, he rarely broke curfew. The few times he had had been for family emergencies.

He turned over and closed his eyes, but images of Lauren earlier with her head thrown back, eyes closed in an expression of pure ecstasy, wouldn't leave him alone. As a result, he tossed and turned all night and, when the alarm went off at five forty-five the next morning, he felt no more rested than he did when he'd lain down the night before.

Malcolm made his usual preworkout smoothie, and by the time he entered the gym, his energy level had climbed a notch or two. He hadn't been this sluggish while working out since the time he'd pulled an all-nighter to study for a kinesiology exam in college. The twenty reps at 225 pounds he normally bench-pressed felt like twice the weight.

"You know, you wouldn't be this tired if you stopped fighting your feelings for a certain dietitian."

He almost dropped the weight. He glared up at Omar. "I don't know what you're talking about." He lifted the weight once more.

Omar waited until Malcolm completed the set. "I'm assuming you're trying to keep you two a secret like Morgan and I did at the beginning of our relationship." Omar had been Morgan's first client when she left her job as an attorney for their family's home safety company and entered the field of sports management. She'd feared that she wouldn't be taken seriously if word got out that she was dating a client.

Malcolm didn't respond.

"If that's the case, you're going to have to do a better job."

He sat up on the bench. "Meaning?"

"Meaning you can't look at her like she's your favorite dessert."

"She just might be," he muttered.

Omar laughed. "That's *exactly* what I told your sister when she said that to me. And you see where we ended up."

He jumped up from the bench and stalked across the gym with Omar's laughter following him. The wide receiver caught up to Malcolm. "Let me know if you want to use my cabin for a short getaway."

Malcolm leaned against the next machine and folded his arms. "I don't even know what I'm doing, Drummond. I shouldn't want to *talk* to her, much less be with her."

"You've been feeling that way since the breakup?"

"No. I'm not going to lie, when it first happened I never wanted to see her again. But it's not like I've spent the last eight years waiting for her or wishing we could get back together." He'd dated, had relationships that lasted for several months and had enjoyed his life. "I didn't feel that anger again until I saw her."

Omar sat and did a set of leg extensions then switched places with Malcolm. He chuckled. "You seemed to have gotten over it pretty easy."

"I don't know about that," he said, gritting his teeth as he lifted the weight.

"In all seriousness, Malcolm, you can't go back. If you want her, you need to let go of the past."

And that was the crux of his problem. He didn't know if he could.

It was easier to keep his feelings and thoughts on lockdown during the weekend practices, when Lauren wasn't at the facility. But Monday morning, she was back with her sensual curves and enticing smile, and Malcolm had to work hard to stay in control. He did a good job keeping his distance for the first half of the week. Other than polite conversation if he passed her in the hallway or the dining room, they had no other contact. By Thursday afternoon, he'd reached his limit. After practice ended, he made his way to her office, praying she didn't have a client. As he rounded the corner, one of his teammates called out to him.

"Hey, Gray. You headed to see Lauren?"

Malcolm glanced over his shoulder at Carlos Jenkins, an offensive lineman. "Yeah. Just need to check in, then I'm headed home. You?"

"Actually, I was going to do the same as you."

He muttered a curse under his breath.

Before the man took a step, his phone rang. He pulled it out and glanced at the display. "Guess I'll talk to Lauren tomorrow. My agent." Carlos answered, nodded Malcolm's way and went in the opposite direction.

Thank goodness. Malcolm reached her open door and stood just outside it watching Lauren for a moment. She sat behind her desk scribbling furiously on a notepad. Her hair partially covered her face, and he couldn't recall seeing anything more alluring. He knocked on the door.

Lauren's head came up and she smiled. "Hey, Malcolm."

Her smile sent a jolt to his midsection. "Got a minute?"

She stood and came around the desk. "Sure. Come on in."

He closed the door and discreetly turned the lock.

"What are you doing?" she asked with a nervous laugh.

"Making sure no one interrupts us." Malcolm crossed the office in three strides, hauled her into his arms and slanted his mouth over hers. What started as a sweet kiss turned hot and demanding in a nanosecond. Lauren slid her hands beneath his shirt, moving them up his abs and chest and driving him insane. She pressed her body closer and he groaned. He was quickly losing control and broke off the kiss.

"I'm not done." Lauren grasped the back of his head and pulled him down for another kiss.

Malcolm was two seconds away from stripping her naked, laying her down on the conference table and burying himself deep inside her until she begged him to stop. "Baby, if you don't want everybody in our business, we need to stop, because I'm about a minute away from taking you on that table over there."

Lauren gasped and nearly jumped out of his arms. "Oh my goodness."

"Hold up a minute," he said, tightening his grip.

She rested her head on his chest. "Somebody could've come in."

He chuckled. "Not unless they can open locked doors."

Her head came up sharply. "What?" She glanced around his shoulder and stared up at him. "You locked the door?"

"I told you I didn't want anyone interrupting us."

She backed out of his hold. "I'm going to have to ban you from my office."

With the erotic fantasies running through his mind at the moment, Malcolm was inclined to agree. Omar's words came back. With his schedule, he wouldn't have time to take a trip up to the cabin, but he needed to figure out a way to get her alone. He didn't have a day off until Sunday. It wasn't soon enough for his tastes, but it would have to do. "What are you doing Sunday afternoon?"

"My friend will be visiting from Phoenix this weekend, but she leaves on Sunday around noon. Why?"

"Just want to spend some time with you. If I pick you up at four, will that give you enough time to do what you need to do for the day?"

Lauren nodded. "It should."

"Good." He leaned down and kissed her softly, being careful not to touch her. It wouldn't take much to send him over the edge. "I'll see you on Sunday."

She reached up and cupped his cheek. "Okay."

The smile she gave him had his heart beating double time. He didn't understand why this one woman affected him so, but his brother-in-law was right about one thing. Malcolm and Lauren couldn't go back, but they could start again, and he knew the perfect way.

Chapter 9

Friday evening, Lauren greeted her parents with strong hugs. "Sorry I'm late. My last appointment ran longer than expected." Christopher Long, the rookie she'd seen with Malcolm, had asked her every question under the sun related to diet, nutrition and the best foods to keep him in peak condition. She appreciated his zeal but thought he could relax a bit.

Her mother waved her off. "Don't worry about it, honey. Come on and get washed up. Dinner is ready."

She hurriedly washed her hands then joined her parents at the table. The aroma from the food made her stomach growl. Lauren tried to practice what she preached when it came to diet and nutrition, but she hadn't eaten her mother's cooking in almost a year and tonight she planned to go all out.

"By the sound of your belly, I guess you're hungry." Her father's deep rumble made her smile.

"Dad, you have no idea. Mom, this smells *so* good. I'm going to try not to hurt myself."

Delores smiled. "I fixed all your favorites, so eat up."

After her father said the blessing, Lauren helped herself to the barbecued chicken, sautéed corn, broccoli with cheese sauce and roasted potatoes. She groaned with every bite. "You outdid yourself, Mom."

"She sure did," Walter said around a mouthful of chicken. They ate in silence for a few minutes. "How are you liking the new job?"

"I love it. Everyone has been so nice, and even though a few of the players complain, I haven't had much trouble. Now that training camp has started, I'm a lot busier."

Her mother reached over and patted her hand. "That's wonderful, sweetheart." She paused. "And Malcolm? I'm sure you've seen him by now."

Lauren had known that would be among the first questions they asked. They understood better than anyone else how devastated she had been over the breakup, particularly since she'd been to blame. Instead of her listening to his explanation and trying to make things right—and Malcolm had made several attempts to talk to her—she'd allowed fear and other people to mess up a beautiful relationship. She speared a piece of broccoli and popped it into her mouth. "Yes, I've seen him."

"And?" her father prompted with his fork. When Lauren didn't answer, he frowned. "Did something happen between you two already?"

Happen? She couldn't begin to describe what was *happening* with her and Malcolm. She had never been so out of control with a man before in her life. *Yes, you have,* that annoying inner voice corrected her. Okay, so she had. Only once. And it was the same man. But she had never done anything so reckless as coming close to having sex at her office. She didn't think it was a good time to share that piece of information.

"No, Daddy. We actually went to dinner the night my car broke down—he was the one who found me on the road—

and we talked. Both of us have grown up, and we're leaving all the rest in the past."

"I'm glad to hear it. You and Malcolm were like two peas in a pod. It's good to see him doing so well in his football career, but the thing that impressed me about him most was that no matter how much sports demanded of him, he never hesitated to leave football on the field and give time to the things that mattered most."

Lauren gave a little laugh. "Wow, Mom. I didn't realize you paid that much attention when he and I were dating."

She smiled knowingly. "I realize more than you're letting on." She lifted her glass of lemonade and took a sip.

What the heck does that mean?

"Finish your food. Didn't you say you had to pick up Valencia from the airport later?"

"Yes." Had Lauren given something away? Mothers always seemed to discern the truth beneath a story, and Delores Emerson was no exception. Lauren went back to eating but pondered her mother's statement for the rest of the visit.

When it came time to leave, her father engulfed her in a comforting hug that let her know he'd be there if and when she needed him. No one gave out hugs like Walter Emerson, and she counted herself blessed to have him in her life. "I love you, Daddy."

"I love you, too. Is the car working out okay?"

She nodded. "It rides like a dream." Despite her protests, he and her mother had gifted her with a new black Acura and told her to think of it as a belated graduation gift to celebrate her master's degree and a congratulations on the new job. Lauren hugged her mom. "Love you, Mom."

"Ditto, baby. And tell Valencia I said hello. If you two aren't too busy tomorrow, I'd love to see her."

"We'll try to stop by after I take her on a tour of the Cobras' practice facility tomorrow."

"All right. You be careful."

"I will." Lauren waved as she got into the car. Before

driving off, she checked to make sure Lyn's plane was on schedule.

She'd forgotten how crazy LAX could be, and all the construction made it worse. She circled twice, had one driver yell and accuse her of driving slowly and another one cut her off and nearly take off the front end of her new car. She finally spotted her friend on the fourth go-around and sent up a silent thank-you. She signaled and eased to the curb.

Valencia threw her bag in the back and got in the front seat. They shared a quick hug. "Hey, girl. It's so good to see you. Nice car."

"You, too, and thanks. The transmission went out on the Maxima and it was cheaper to buy a new one." Lauren checked the traffic before merging. "How was the flight?"

"It was fine. Oh, guess who asked about you today as I was leaving?"

"Who?"

"Jeffrey."

Lauren gave a quick roll of her eyes at the mention of her ex. "Why is he asking about me? He didn't say two words to me the last three months I was there."

"I have no idea. He said he hadn't seen you around and wanted to know if you were okay. I think he was fishing for information. Information I didn't give him," she added with a laugh. "All he knows is that you don't work there anymore."

"And that's all he needs to know." Aside from her supervisor and Lyn, Lauren hadn't told anyone else where she would be working—just that she had a dream opportunity. She wasn't naive enough to believe people wouldn't find out sooner or later. A woman entering a male-dominated field most always made the news. She just wanted to fly under the radar for as long as possible, especially now that she had agreed to date Malcolm. The media would have a field day with that piece of news.

"You're still taking me to tour the Cobras' practice facility tomorrow, right?"

Lauren chuckled. "It's either that or you'll bug me to death."

"Please, *please* tell me the team will be practicing."

She slanted her friend an amused glance. "Yeah, they'll be practicing."

Valencia pumped her fists in the air. "Yes, baby! I have to make sure my phone is fully charged. I don't want to miss one photo op." She bounced in her seat. "Wait. Do you think any of them will pose for pictures?"

"I have no idea, but you can ask."

"I think it'll be better coming from you," she said sweetly.

"Mmm-hmm."

After they got to Lauren's condo, the two spent the rest of the evening laughing, eating their favorite cookies-and-cream ice cream, and catching up.

Valencia yawned. "I am so tired. I worked ten hours today and went straight to the airport from the hospital."

"Were you covering for someone?"

"Yep. The new dietitian was out sick, so I saw three of her patients after I finished with mine."

Lauren stood. "Well, let me show you where everything is so you can go to bed."

Valencia slowly got to her feet and trudged down the hallway behind Lauren. "I really like your place."

"Thanks." Lauren pointed out the cabinet holding the towels. "If you need anything else, I'll be in my room. Otherwise, I'll see you in the morning." They shared another hug. "I'm so glad you're here."

"Me, too. You get a pass for the night on Malcolm, because I'm too tired and I need to be fully alert for this update. But I expect *all* the details tomorrow."

Lauren smiled and shook her head. "Figured as much. Good night."

"'Night."

Lauren had planned to sleep in until at least ten, but Valencia was up at nine the next morning, standing in Lauren's bedroom door asking when they'd be leaving. They got to the facility at ten, instead of at eleven thirty, like she had intended.

They stopped at the security desk to get a visitor's badge before beginning the tour, and Valencia's eyes were wide as she followed Lauren around the facility.

"This is *fantastic*! I see why you got lost. You've turned down so many hallways, I have no idea which way is which."

"I told you." She stopped at her office, unlocked the door and gestured her in with a flourish. "My office."

"Wow. You have moved up, girlfriend. Don't you need help? I'm more than willing to relocate." She walked over to the large window. "And look at this view. Those gardens are beautiful."

Lauren came to stand next to Valencia. "They are. I try to go walking on the path as often as I can, which hasn't been much since training camp started."

"Speaking of…"

"Yeah, I know. You want to go watch practice. You are way too excited."

"You got that right. Who wouldn't be excited about seeing a bunch of sexy guys in those tight-fitting athletic outfits with muscles flexing and all glistening from sweat…?"

"You are truly crazy, girl. Come on. I want to introduce you to Nigel, who's the chef, and then we'll head out to the practice field."

Valencia did a little shimmy and rubbed her hands together with glee.

They found Nigel in the kitchen with his team, deep into the lunch prep. The fruit and salad stations had been filled and the warmers turned on and awaiting whatever selections were on the day's menu. Two of the kitchen staff had blenders going, making the recovery smoothies for players to have when practice ended in half an hour. They'd have about an hour to consume the drink and shower before heading to their respective team meetings.

"Hey, Lauren," Nigel said, his eyes widening in surprise. "What are you doing here?"

"Hi, Nigel. My friend Valencia is visiting from Phoenix, and I'm showing her around."

"Nice to meet you, Valencia. I'd shake your hand, but as you can see, mine are a little messy right now." He had on a pair of gloves and was seasoning a tub of chicken breasts.

Valencia laughed. "It's no problem, and it's nice to meet you, as well."

Not wanting to interrupt his flow, Lauren said, "We'll get out of your hair. See you on Monday."

"Enjoy your weekend, ladies. Wish I could be enjoying it with you," he added with a smile.

They both laughed and left him to his work. Lauren led Valencia down two hallways and out a back door and tunnel that led to the field.

Valencia stood as if starstruck. "Lord, have mercy. Have you ever seen such a glorious sight?" she whispered in awe.

Lauren had to agree. The men were impressive. There were several drills going on in various areas, but she only had eyes for one player. She observed Malcolm practicing taking handoffs from the quarterback and running various patterns.

"You are in so much trouble, Lauren."

She shifted her gaze to Lyn. "What do you mean?"

"Malcolm is even finer than he was in college, and his body…my, my, my."

Yeah, she was in trouble. Big trouble.

"I think I'm ready for the 411 now. And by the look on your face, a whole lot more has happened."

"You don't know the half of it." Lauren told her about Malcolm coming to her rescue the day her car broke down, the dinner where they cleared the air and the subsequent kisses. "The other day, he came to my office, and I was this close to having sex with him right there." She held her thumb and index finger together.

Valencia's eyes went wide. "Are you *serious*?" she squealed, then slapped a hand over her mouth. She repeated the question, but this time quieter.

Lauren ran a hand over her forehead. "There's more. He wants us to see each other again."

"And you said?"

"Definitely not what I should have." She'd been wrestling with her decision for the past few days but couldn't force herself to walk away.

"Which means yes."

Lauren nodded. "And he asked me to spend the day with him tomorrow after you leave." A wide smile spread across Valencia's face, and warning bells sounded in Lauren's head. "What are you thinking?"

"That after I get my pictures, we're going shopping to get you something cute to wear tomorrow." Valencia winked and turned her attention back to the field. "Who are those two brothers that just ran by?"

"They're the wide receivers. Marcus Dupree, and the one with the locs is Omar Drummond. And he's married... to Malcolm's twin sister."

"I'm guessing they hooked up because of her brother?"

"Nope. From what I understand, their relationship started after he asked her to be his agent. She worked as an attorney for the Gray family's company, initially."

"I am *so* in the wrong field. Maybe I need to check out the requirements to be an agent."

Lauren burst out laughing. A few minutes later, practice ended. Several of the guys called out greetings to Lauren and were more than willing to pose for photos.

"Hey, Lauren," Malcolm said, stopping in front of them. His eyes held hers for the briefest moment, but long enough to send heat flowing through her body. "Hey. I don't know if you remember my friend from school."

"I do. Good to see you, Valencia."

"Same here." She held up her phone. "You mind?"

"Not at all." He stood next to Valencia and smiled as she snapped the photo.

"Thanks, Malcolm."

"You're welcome. I'll see you later." He spoke to Valencia, but his gaze was focused on Lauren.

As soon as he was out of earshot, Valencia said, "I predict that the two of you will be engaged before the football season is over." She pointed a finger Lauren's way. "And this time, neither one of you better mess it up."

Lauren whipped her head around, praying no one else had heard. "Let's go, Miss Trouble."

"Yes, let's. We have some shopping to do. A lovely sundress that shows off your curves and a little leg will be perfect." She grabbed Lauren's arm and ushered her back the way they'd come.

She tried to ignore her friend's outrageous prediction, but the words stayed with Lauren for the rest of the day. And as crazy as it sounded, secretly the thought thrilled her.

Saturday evening, Malcolm lay on the floor in Siobhan and Justin's family room tossing his niece into the air and listening to her delighted squeals. He had been worried about his sister since the episode at their parents' house the previous week. Although he had called to check on her, he needed to see for himself how she was doing.

"How's work?" Siobhan worked as the PR director for their family's company.

Siobhan chuckled. "It's work. I've had to stay late a couple of days because we're getting ready to launch Justin's in-home alert system, and you know I have to make sure my baby gets maximum exposure." Justin had partnered with the company to manufacture his new product.

With the use of sensors placed around the home, real-time data could be sent directly to a smartphone from a wireless hub—whether a door had been left open, a stove left on, or if a person hadn't moved in hours—that allowed elderly relatives to remain at home and gave caregivers peace of mind.

Malcolm glanced over at her. "Yeah, I bet." He hesitated asking, but he wanted to know. "Any word on when Christian can come to stay permanently?"

She brightened. "The social worker called yesterday and said we could bring him home in two weeks, tops. Justin and I are going to take off that first week so we can get him enrolled in preschool and generally try to make the transition easy for him. He's been bounced around so much since his parents died two years ago it makes my heart hurt."

He sat up, cradled Nyla in his arms and handed her a book. "What happened to them?"

"From what we were told, they died when the party yacht they were on was struck by another boat," Justin said. "The guys on the other boat had been drinking and lost control."

Malcolm shook his head. "I don't know what I'd do if we lost Mom and Dad now, so I can't even imagine how it is for Christian." He instinctively held Nyla closer.

Siobhan nodded. "He doesn't remember them, really, just that they were gone and not coming back. And that's why Justin and I are going to make sure he gets all the love he deserves. He's such a sweet little boy."

Nyla decided she'd had enough of being held and squirmed until Malcolm set her on her feet. She smiled at him and opened and closed her hand repeatedly. When he didn't move, she started to whine and did it again. Malcolm's brows knit in confusion. "Sorry, baby girl, Uncle Malcolm doesn't know what that means. Vonnie?"

She chuckled. "She wants some milk. Lexia taught us

some baby signs so Nyla can communicate with us instead of crying every time she wants something."

Because her best friend had lost her hearing as a teen, Lexia had learned sign language. Malcolm would always be grateful to his sister-in-law for helping Khalil through his ordeal. "That is so cool. What else does she know?"

"More, all done and eat," Justin said with a laugh.

"Hey, well, she's got all the important ones." When Nyla made the sign again, Siobhan stood, picked up her daughter and went into the kitchen.

"Justin, how is Vonnie really doing?" he asked quietly.

Justin leaned forward. "Sunday and Monday were rough, man. You know how strong she always is, but this time…" He trailed off, and Malcolm could see the agony reflected in his face. "Hearing her cry felt like my heart was being ripped from my chest, and I couldn't do anything about it. I felt so damn helpless. But she's handling it better now, and knowing we only have a week or so before Christian will be here permanently has helped."

He felt his own emotions rising. "I hope the time passes quickly." Though Siobhan was six years older, Malcolm was still very close to his sister. All of his siblings maintained a rare bond that had grown stronger as they gotten older. It had been hard for him and his brothers to relinquish responsibility for Siobhan and Morgan's well-being to their husbands, but both couldn't have found better partners. He checked the time. "I need to get going."

On the heels of his words, Siobhan came back with Nyla and her sippy cup filled with milk. "Since you're off tomorrow, you're welcome to come by for dinner."

"Sounds good, but I already have plans."

"Plans that no doubt include Lauren, correct?" she asked pointedly.

"Yes."

"Well, you might not want to hear what I have to say, but I'm going to say it anyway."

He rolled his eyes and steeled himself for her speech about how he needed to be careful and not get too caught up.

"I know she messed up things between you two years ago. We all made stupid mistakes when we were young. I also know that, although you've moved on, you still have feelings for her. I believe she's the one for you, Malcolm."

For a moment, Malcolm sat stunned. When he finally found his voice, he asked, "And why do you think that?"

"Simple. She's the only woman who has ever owned your heart." Siobhan waved a hand. "Yeah, yeah, you've dated other women, and I'm not saying you weren't happy with them. You were. But none of them could make your eyes light up the way they do when you're around Lauren. I saw you two dancing at the awards dinner."

He divided his gaze between his sister and brother-in-law.

Justin smiled. "Big sister has spoken."

Malcolm pushed to his feet. "On that note, I'm outta here." He kissed Nyla, and she stopped drinking her milk long enough to give him a wet one of her own. He pressed a kiss to Siobhan's temple. "See you later, sis."

Justin walked him to the door. "Since we're passing out unwanted advice, I'll just add if you plan to pursue Lauren, be ready to go the distance, no matter what."

"Thanks." He didn't know if he was ready to go the distance, only that he wanted her now.

Chapter 10

Lauren opened the door to Malcolm Sunday afternoon a few minutes before four. He was dressed casually in shorts and a pullover tee. "Hi. Come in." Malcolm didn't move. His gaze made a slow tour from her sandaled feet to her face. She would have to be blind not to see the naked desire in his eyes. The appreciative gleam in his eyes let her know that the purple halter sundress was a good choice.

"Um…you never said where we're going, so I didn't know what to wear. Is this okay?"

"It's better than okay." He kissed her lightly. "And I don't think I should come in. If I do, we aren't leaving."

Her breath caught. She had no problem interpreting his meaning. And she wouldn't protest if they didn't. "Let me get my purse."

Once on the road, he said, "I really like the dress."

"Thank you."

"Did Lyn get home okay?"

She smiled at his use of Valencia's nickname. "Yes. She

sent me a text. I want to thank you and the guys for being so gracious yesterday. She was beside herself with excitement."

"I could tell."

"You never said where we're going."

"My place."

Lauren didn't know where she'd expected them to go—a movie, early dinner or something—but his house? After what happened in her office, he'd only have to suggest going farther and she'd agree. It was only a matter of time before they had sex, and she didn't know if she would be able to separate her emotions from the physical aspects. She never had. Not with him.

"Are you okay with it?"

She rotated in his direction. "Yes."

"I hope you don't mind starting so early."

"Not at all. I know you have a curfew, even if they don't enforce it. I think it says a lot about your integrity and commitment." She'd read lots of stories of athletes hanging out late and getting into trouble and respected Malcolm even more, because not once in all the years that he'd been playing football had she read or seen one bad thing about him. "Besides, I have to go to work tomorrow, too."

"Speaking of work, it seems like you're settling in well. The guys all speak highly of you. The veterans are glad to have someone there who's about helping the players be better instead of trying to make a profit."

"I'm glad to hear it. Of course, there are a few who aren't too happy with the changes I'm suggesting, but I knew it wouldn't be an easy road. And I'm hoping this will help with the book I'm writing."

"If you need any help or information, let me know."

"Seriously?"

"Of course," he chuckled.

If she could get a testimonial from Malcolm attesting to the fact that her methods were sound, or even a quote, it would be a huge boost. "I hope you know that I will be taking you up on that offer."

"I hope you do."

When they arrived at his house, he parked in the garage and took her in through the door that connected to his laundry room. She hadn't seen it her first time here, but just like everything else, the washer and dryer were state-of-the-art. The room had plenty of cabinet space and a counter, which she assumed could be used for folding clothes.

"Go on into the family room and I'll be there in a minute," he said.

Lauren went through the kitchen and stopped in her tracks upon seeing a large blanket spread out on the family room floor. Something about it seemed familiar. She moved closer and brought her hand to her mouth. It was same blanket they'd picnicked on in his apartment nearly ten years ago. They had planned to go to a park but had to alter their plans due to a surprise spring storm. She couldn't believe he'd kept it all this time. Her gaze went to the deck of cards in the center. She recalled with vivid clarity what happened the last time they'd played, and just the thought made her nipples harden and the space between her thighs throb.

"I thought we'd have a picnic," Malcolm said, entering with a basket similar to the one they had used before.

"What are you...why the picnic?"

He placed the basket on the edge of the blanket and framed her face in his hands. "You said we couldn't go back, and I agree. But we can start over. And this was the start of everything good between us. I want it to be better this time." He touched his mouth to hers.

"I want it to be better, too."

"Then we're in agreement, sunshine."

He kissed her with a tenderness that almost melted her on the spot, and the long-forgotten endearment went straight to her heart. When she had asked why he called her that the first time, he said her smile was like pure sunshine.

Malcolm kicked off his shoes and gestured for her to take a seat.

She sat, removed her sandals, tucked her legs beneath her to one side and smoothed her dress down.

He lowered himself next to her and unearthed two plates, two coasters and two champagne glasses. "I figure this time we can have a little champagne to celebrate," he said wryly, opening a bottle.

Lauren chuckled. The first time, they'd had sparkling cider because both of them were just shy of their twenty-first birthdays. "Yeah, I think we could pass for legal." She held up the glasses, and he filled them.

He set the bottle aside, accepted his glass from her and held it up. "To starting over and doing it better."

"To starting over and doing it better." She touched his glass and took a sip. "So, what are we having?"

A secretive smile curved his lips. "A little of this and a little of that."

"What are you up to?"

Malcolm reached inside the basket and took out three containers. "Open them."

Lauren removed the tops of the containers and gasped. Her gaze flew to his. He had recreated the meal—fried chicken wings, raw carrots and celery, and strawberries, mangoes and grapes. "You remembered what we ate."

"It's not something I've ever forgotten."

She searched his face, trying to figure out what he meant.

"You go first." He handed her a plate and napkin. "And this isn't going to get me into trouble with the team dietitian, is it?"

"I'll talk to her, but I'm sure she won't mind one splurge meal." They shared a smile. She filled her plate and waited while he did his own. He grasped her hand and recited a short blessing. She decided to start with the chicken wing.

"I haven't fried chicken in I don't know how long, so I hope it tastes okay."

"I remember how well you cook, so I'm not worried at all." Lauren moaned with the first bite. It tasted even better than she remembered. "This is so good! I could eat these every day."

Malcolm chuckled. "That's what you used to say. And then you said if you gained weight, it would be my fault."

"Yeah, well… I have gained a few pounds over the years," she said, smiling.

"And they're in all the right places, trust me. The guys on the team can't seem to take their eyes off you every time you enter the room."

The tone in his voice gave her pause. "You almost sound like you're jealous or something."

All playfulness fled. "Do I need to be?"

She met his serious eyes. "No." Since that kiss in her office, she hadn't thought of any other man.

Malcolm dipped a carrot in ranch dressing and popped into his mouth. "Good to know."

They ate in silence for a few minutes, but every time Lauren glanced his way, she found him staring. "Is something wrong?"

"Not at all. Everything's perfect." He leaned over and pressed a soft kiss behind her ear.

When they finished eating, she pointed to the cards. "You still have the same deck."

He shrugged. "No need to throw them away. I pull them out every now and again to play solitaire when I'm trying to clear my head. You want anything else?"

"No, thanks."

"We'll have dessert later." He repacked the basket and moved it aside. "But right now," he said, picking up the cards and shuffling them, "we're going to play."

Lauren grinned. "And as I recall, I wiped the floor with you in gin rummy."

He wiggled his eyebrows. "At first."

Her heart rate spiked. The last time they'd played, the bet started with pennies, but when she won nearly every hand, he'd upped the ante to articles of clothing. Lauren had done well and had him almost naked—until the last two hands. He took sweet revenge, and it turned out to be the most erotic game of cards she had ever played. Today, she had on only three things—her dress, bra and panties—which meant she couldn't afford to lose even one hand.

"Um… Malcolm, we're not going to bet… I don't think—"

"Nope. We're not betting articles of clothing."

She relaxed.

"Something better."

"What?"

Malcolm scooted closer until they were only a breath apart. "Kisses," he murmured against her lips. "Every spread counts as one kiss, and we pay up at the end of each game. Deal?"

Confident in her skill and the fact that it was only kisses, she stuck out her hand. "Deal." In the recesses of her mind, that little caution signal reminded her about the effects his kisses had on her and that, more than likely, the end result would be the same. *Kissgasm.* He dealt the first hand, and Lauren smiled inwardly at her cards. He wouldn't be getting one kiss.

"Let's see whatcha got, sunshine."

She drew a card. "Oh, you'll see, angel eyes." The name tumbled out before she could stop it. She took a wary glance his way to gauge his reaction.

He smiled. "Haven't heard that in a while. Just make sure you don't say it when we're at the office," he added with a wink.

"Shut up," she said, rolling her eyes and spreading three matches.

"Oh, the girl thinks she still got a little game, huh?"

"A little? Baby, I got more game than you know."

Malcolm's hand paused on the deck. "Is that right? Hmm... I'm definitely up for that."

His expression said he was talking about more than a card game. She had slipped back into their old banter without missing a beat. In the past, she wouldn't have hesitated to play these sensual games, but tonight the sexual tension between them was so thick that they'd be in his bed if she gave the slightest hint she was ready to take the next step. Her mind said it might be too soon, but her body disagreed. And to prove its point, a sweet ache spread between her legs.

Malcolm threw out a card.

Two rounds later, Lauren laid out two more spreads. "Gin." She smiled serenely. "Well, I guess that means five kisses for me and..." She spread her hands. "None for you."

He leaned back on his elbows. "Then I'm at your mercy."

She hesitantly rose to her knees, braced one hand on the blanket next to him and kissed his temple. He raised an eyebrow, but she ignored it. "One." She kissed his cheek, and then his lips briefly, twice.

"I thought you said you had game."

She put her hand on her hips. "What? You saying you don't like my kisses?"

"When you kiss me, I'll let you know. I think you have one more," he said with a challenge in his eyes.

Lauren had never backed down from a challenge and leaned forward. She nibbled his bottom lip and slid her tongue inside, capturing his and taking her time reacquainting herself with the taste that was uniquely him. He reached up to cup the back of her head to hold her in place, and she broke off the kiss. "Five. How's that?"

His eyes remained closed for a moment. "Not bad, but I think we need to play another game to be sure." Malcolm gathered up the cards and placed them in front of her. "Your deal."

That last kiss had tested her resolve and she was tempted to toss the cards, knock him backward and straddle him then and there. She shuffled the deck and dealt another hand. Turning over her cards, Lauren noted that it wouldn't be as easy this game. She only hoped Malcolm's hand was as bad as hers. If he ended up winning, she could call it a wrap on her control.

His face was unreadable as he drew the first card. He studied his hand for a moment, then discarded another one. "Problems?" he asked with amusement.

"Nope." She took her turn. Midway through the game, she was up four to two and felt confident in winning and in her ability to control the rising heat.

Malcolm took his turn, smiled then counted, including the two he already had, "One, two, three, four, five, six…gin."

Lauren's mouth dropped. "How did you do that?"

"Skill, baby. Now…" A wicked smile spread across his face. "I believe it's time to show you *my* game."

Uh-oh.

He rose on all fours and came to her slowly, as if sizing up his prey, his smile still in place. "Mmm…where to start…"

"What do—" The feel of his mouth on her bare shoulder stole the rest of her words.

"One." He eased back a fraction. "I think I like this game a lot better than strip gin rummy. What about you?"

"When you kiss me, I'll let you know," she said, repeating his earlier words.

Malcolm angled his head thoughtfully. "Oh, I'm going to kiss you, all right." He moved over her until she was lying flat on her back. "Baby, I'm going to kiss you in ways and in places you've never been kissed," he said in a heated rush, holding her gaze.

His words shattered what little control she had left. She wanted this man, plain and simple. "Then kiss me, Malcolm." Without waiting, she grabbed his head and crushed her mouth against his. He wasted no time taking over the kiss and making her senses spin.

At length, he raised his head. "Are you trying to steal my kisses?"

"Can't steal something you haven't given."

Surprise lit his eyes. "Well, I'd better remedy that right now. And that one didn't count as one of mine." He slid down her body and pushed her dress up to her waist, caressing from the ankle to the upper thigh of one leg, then the other.

Lauren could barely breathe. He snaked his tongue up her inner thigh, stopping mere inches from her center, and placed a lingering kiss there. She had no doubt he knew how wet she was. When he kissed the other thigh, her legs began to shake.

"Three more to go. Hmm…where should I go next?"

She didn't care, as long as he didn't stop. He grazed her core as he made his way up to her belly button and swirled his tongue around, eliciting a loud moan.

"I take that to mean my kisses are getting better. What about this one?" Malcolm asked, releasing the tie on her dress and freeing her breasts. He pushed them together and suckled both nipples.

Her breath came in short gasps. "Mal… Malcolm…"

He dragged his body along hers until they were face-to-face and braced himself on his forearms. "What is it, sweetheart?"

Lauren was so on fire, one more touch and she'd go up in flames. He reclaimed her mouth in a slow, drugging kiss. Then he changed the tempo. His tongue thrust deeply, plunging in and out as if he were making love to her and sending shock waves straight to her core. She tore her mouth away and screamed his name as a blinding orgasm ripped through her. She shuddered and sucked in a deep breath, trying to force air into her lungs. Malcolm had always been attentive to her needs when they had sex, but never in her life had she come just from kissing. She opened her eyes and saw him above her with a pleased male smile.

"Like I said...in places and ways you've never been kissed. And we're just getting started." Malcolm scooped her into his arms, stood, carried her up to his bedroom and placed her in the center of his bed.

Chapter 11

Malcolm stared at the alluring picture Lauren made lying in his bed with her dress half-on—her bra pulled down, dress up around her waist. He didn't think he could get any harder. He never brought women to his home, because he always worried that his address would end up being blasted through social media or he'd find groupies camped out in his yard later.

His last relationship had ended at the beginning of the year—the woman had taken exception to the fact that she wouldn't be accompanying him on his monthlong vacation—and he'd been content not to date. Until now. He found it ironic that Lauren would be the first woman he brought to his house. And regardless of how this turned out, he trusted that she would never divulge any of his personal information.

Lauren sat up on her elbows. "Are you going to stand there all evening? It's almost eight o'clock, and you do have a curfew."

He laughed softly and climbed onto the bed. "We have

Dear Reader,

IT'S A FACT: if you answer 4 quick questions, we'll send you **4 FREE REWARDS!**

I'm not kidding you. As a leading publisher of women's fiction, we value your opinions... and your time. That's why we are prepared to **reward** you handsomely for completing our mini-survey. In fact, we have 4 Free Rewards for you, including 2 free books and 2 free gifts.

As you may have guessed, that's why our mini-survey is called **"4 for 4".** Answer 4 questions and get 4 Free Rewards. It's that simple!

Thank you for participating in our survey,

Pam Powers

To get your 4 FREE REWARDS:
Complete the survey below and return the insert today to receive 2 FREE BOOKS and 2 FREE GIFTS guaranteed!

"4 for 4" MINI-SURVEY

1 Is reading one of your favorite hobbies?

☐ YES ☐ NO

2 Do you prefer to read instead of watch TV?

☐ YES ☐ NO

3 Do you read newspapers and magazines?

☐ YES ☐ NO

4 Do you enjoy trying new book series with FREE BOOKS?

☐ YES ☐ NO

YES! I have completed the above Mini-Survey. Please send me my 4 FREE REWARDS (worth over $20 retail). I understand that I am under no obligation to buy anything, as explained on the back of this card.

168/368 XDL GMYK

FIRST NAME	LAST NAME

ADDRESS

APT.#	CITY

STATE/PROV.	ZIP/POSTAL CODE

© 2017 HARLEQUIN ENTERPRISES LIMITED
® and ™ are trademarks owned and used by the trademark owner and/or its licensee. Printed in the U.S.A.
K-218-MS17

READER SERVICE—Here's how it works:

plenty of time." He lowered himself half on top of her, being careful not to place his full weight on her, and locked his mouth on hers. Sensations he'd tried to keep at bay came back full force. He'd spent the last two weeks wanting Lauren this way, and no amount of reasoning had taken away the longing. He stripped off her dress and laid it on the bench at the foot of the bed. Next came the strapless deep purple bra and matching bikini panties. "I like these." He remembered that she had always liked matching her underwear. He liked them, too. So much so that he had accompanied her to Victoria's Secret on more than one occasion, picked out and paid for his favorites.

"I know. That's why I wore them."

"And you knew we'd end up here."

"Without a doubt," Lauren said, leaning up to kiss him. She grabbed the hem of his shirt and pulled it up and over his head. She ran her palms over his chest and arms. "Mmm, even better than I remember."

Malcolm sucked in a sharp breath when he felt her warm tongue circling around his nipples. Her hands went to his belt buckle and, with deft fingers, undid it and his pants in a matter of seconds. He raised himself up to facilitate their removal. He sat up and let his gaze roam over her nakedness, noting the slight changes. She had maintained her slender frame, but her breasts were slightly fuller and her hips wider. Malcolm closed his eyes and used his hands to chart a path from her feet, up her toned, honey-brown legs and thighs, and over her hips. He paused a moment to stroke her wet center, then continued his journey upward to her breasts. Lauren's soft moans filled his ears and aroused him to a level he hadn't experienced in a long time, if ever.

She reached between them, grasped his engorged shaft and slid her hand up and down his length. "Stop teasing me."

He clamped down on her hand almost immediately. The pressure of her hand on him, coupled with the fact that he hadn't had sex in almost five months, had him just this side of exploding. "Don't do that," he gritted out.

"Do what?" she asked sultrily, still rubbing her thumb under the head.

Trying to maintain control, Malcolm carefully disengaged her hand and left briefly to don a condom, then came back to the bed. "You were never this playful before."

Lauren shifted beneath him until he fit snugly at her center. "Like I said before, I've changed."

"Let's see how much." Using his knee, he spread her legs and eased his way inside. She was so tight he glanced up questioningly.

A faint smile touched her lips. "It's been a while."

As irrational as it might seem to expect that she hadn't slept with another man in eight years, he felt a quick flash of jealousy. Determined to make her forget every other man except him, he met her eyes and started with slow, deep thrusts. A familiar emotion welled up, but he pushed it down and concentrated only on drawing out as much pleasure as he could from this interlude.

She locked her legs around his back and tilted her hips to meet his strokes, while her hands reached for his head. "I miss your locs," she murmured.

A vision of her gripping his hair as she came surfaced and made him increase the tempo. Her walls clamped down on him, and he gritted his teeth to keep from coming. "Damn, baby. You feel so good."

"Mmm, so do you."

Automatically, Malcolm tilted her hips higher, knowing it would increase the sensations.

Lauren arched and let out a long moan. "Malcolm, *Malcolm!*"

"Right here, sunshine," he murmured against her ear, pumping faster. He felt her tiny contractions, signaling her release was near, and slowed his movements. "Look at me, sweetheart. I want to see your eyes when you come." He rotated his hips in a circular motion, plunging with deep, measured strokes. Her expression of sheer ecstasy mirrored what he felt. Malcolm was close, and he wanted them to come together. "Come for me, Lauren." He pulled back and drove inside with one hard thrust, and she screamed. His orgasm roared through him with such force, it left him gasping for air. Their bodies shook and shuddered for what seemed like forever before their breathing slowed. He placed a gentle kiss on her lips and rolled to his side, taking her with him.

She lay facing him with her leg thrown over his and her head on his chest. "So, who won?"

"Technically I did, since I had six to your five, but I'm willing to call it a draw," he said with a chuckle. "I do think my kisses were better than yours, though."

Her head popped up, and she punched him playfully. "I beg your pardon."

He angled his head and raised a brow. "You can beg all you like, but weren't you the one who had an orgasm downstairs?"

Lauren dropped her head. "That's never happened before."

"And I've never done it to anyone before."

He felt her smile. "Then we can keep the kissgasm between us."

Malcolm laughed. "*Kissgasm?* That's not even a word."

"It is now. Next time, we'll see if I can't give you one. I'm certain there are a few places I can kiss that will produce the desired effects."

He grew hard again with just the thought.

She stroked a finger down his chest to his abdomen. "Like somewhere along here, or—" she skimmed a hand over his rising erection "—here, maybe. What do you think?"

His stomach clenched. "I think if you keep that up, you're going to be in trouble." Malcolm glimpsed at the clock on his nightstand. As much as he wanted to go a second round, it would have to wait. They still had to shower and he had to drive Lauren home. "Unfortunately, we'll have to take a rain check." He kissed her forehead, sighed deeply and swung his legs over the side of the bed. "Come on, let's go take a shower."

"Together?" she asked warily.

"Yeah. I'll behave, even though I don't want to."

Afterward, he drove her home and walked her to the door. "I gotta tell you, baby, I'm going to have a hard time ignoring you tomorrow."

Lauren came up on tiptoe and kissed him. "You don't have to ignore me. You can say hello."

He swatted her playfully on the butt. "Sassy woman. You know what I mean."

"I do, and I'm going to have a hard time, too," she confessed.

He opened his mouth to tell her they didn't have to pretend, but closed it. He knew how hard it was to land this type of job and wanted her to succeed, so he respected her enough to wait. Besides, the first preseason game would be next weekend, and he needed to keep his head clear. He couldn't afford a distraction this late in his career.

Lauren had a much harder time masking her feelings for Malcolm than she'd anticipated. By Wednesday, she had taken to avoiding him, because each time she saw him, it took every ounce of control she possessed not to plant her lips on his. He seemed to have an easier time, barely acknowledging her when their paths crossed. But this was what she'd asked for, so she had to deal with it.

Turning to her computer, she logged on to her Twitter account. She followed a number of the players and found many of their tweets hilarious. Her hand paused on the track pad when she saw a tweet from Brent. He'd posted before and after photos of his previous night's dinner. The former showed a large sub sandwich, a whole pizza loaded with toppings, a family-size bag of barbecue chips and a two-liter of Coke. The latter showed empty packaging and bottle, with the words Best dinner ever!

Lauren replied to his tweet with I guess I'll be seeing you in my office this week, along with a frowning emoji and photos of lean meats, fruits and vegetables. She knew he'd seen her reply when she passed him on his way to the dining room after practice and he wouldn't meet her eyes. She sent him an email with an appointment for Friday after practice.

She spent the remainder of the day compiling information on those players whose body composition measurements had been done recently and comparing them with the previous tests. All of the players would have their testing done over the course of the next week, and she would adjust eating plans accordingly, if necessary.

Friday afternoon, Brent sat across from her desk sulking. He had weighed in three pounds heavier than the last time.

"I can't even get a cheat meal?" he complained.

"Of course you can, Brent. But the fact that you've gained weight despite the heavy workout schedule tells me you're cheating more often than not." She sighed. "Look, I'm not going to police your eating habits, but know that I also will *not* report anything to management but the truth. You're just starting in the league, and you've worked hard to get here. I'm sure you don't want to jeopardize any chance you have to stay here."

Brent slumped down in the chair. "No, I don't. I just like to eat."

Lauren smiled. "I understand. Let's see if we can't incorporate a few lower-fat versions of your favorite foods so that you're staying within your daily caloric limits… say, maybe once or twice a week."

A smile blossomed on his handsome tanned face. "Like brownies and chips?"

"Yes. I'm sure we can find a few recipes or ready-made options." An hour later, they'd come up with a workable meal plan. He stood, and she followed suit. "I'll see you in two weeks to check your progress, but if you have any questions or problems, call or email me."

"I will. Thanks, Lauren."

Before she could blink, he wrapped her in a hug that lifted her off her feet. "Whoa."

A tinge of red colored his cheeks, and he offered up an embarrassed smile. "Sorry."

"No apology necessary. I'll see you later."

He nodded and left.

Lauren was still standing in the same spot with a smile on her face when Darren knocked. "Come on in, Darren. How's it going?"

Darren grinned. "It's going great. Have you seen my latest numbers?" By the perspiration dotting his forehead and damp clothing, he had obviously come straight from practice.

"I have, and you're down fifteen pounds in five weeks."

"So, if I keep doing what I'm doing, I should be able to make my weight goals, right?"

"I think so."

"I talked to Coach, and he said I have a good chance. Oh, my girlfriend is really proud of me and said it's helping her eat healthier, too. On my days off, I eat a little bit less but still go running."

"Sounds like you've got a good handle on things, Darren."

"I couldn't have done it without your help."

"I appreciate that, but you're the one who did all the work." His praise was one more reason why taking this job had been a good idea. The preseason started next weekend, and she had no doubts that Darren would be back to his ideal weight well before the regular season.

"I won't hold you. I need to shower before dinner."

"Okay. Why don't you check in with me in a couple of weeks?"

"Will do." He departed with a smile.

Lauren made a few more notes, including some she planned to use in her book, and packed up to leave.

"Hey, baby."

She whirled around at the sound of Malcolm's voice. Her heart rate kicked up. Because of their schedules, they hadn't spoken other than a few text messages and two brief phone calls, and she had missed him. He stood leaning against the closed door dressed in basketball shorts and a sleeveless fitness tee. "Hey yourself." She crossed the floor, wrapped her arms around his waist and laid her head on his chest. She heard the strong, rhythmic sound of his heartbeat beneath her ear. "It's been a busy week."

Malcolm gathered her closer and dropped a kiss on her temple. "It has, and we have a late night tonight—watching films after dinner."

A twinge of disappointment hit her. She had hoped they would be able to spend a couple of hours together tonight.

He must have sensed it, because he said, "I'm disappointed, too, but I'll make up for it."

She lifted her eyes to meet his. "It's okay. I understand." And she did. It had been the same when they were in college, and she couldn't fault him for doing his job.

"We're done at three tomorrow, but my sister-in-law is having a book signing, and I promised to attend. I have next Tuesday off, so maybe we can sneak in a few hours after you get off."

"That would be great. What kind of book did she write?"

"A cookbook for teens and college students."

Lauren smiled. "With the way college students eat, her book should fly off the shelves."

He buried his face in her neck and kissed her. "She's hoping so. What are you going to be doing?"

"I'm going to spend time working on my book."

"I know you said it was going to be about nutrition for athletes, but what kinds of things are you including?"

"Some basic nutrition guidelines, the science behind it and then, more specifically, how nutrition impacts performance. I'm hoping a couple of the guys on the team will allow me to use a quote or two."

"I'm sure they will, and I'll do one, too, if it'll help."

"Aw, thank you, baby. But don't you think people will say you're biased?"

He shrugged. "I won't be lying, so…"

He slanted his mouth over hers, and Lauren gave herself up to the sensations flowing through her. It felt like ages since he'd last kissed her, and although they probably shouldn't be doing this in her office, she wanted every second of what he gave her.

At length, Malcolm lifted his head. "I need to get out of here while I still can. Be careful going home and text me when you get there."

"Okay."

"I'll call you tomorrow night."

She leaned up and kissed him once more. "Talk to you tomorrow."

He opened the door, smiled and gave her hand a gentle squeeze.

A moment later she heard him talking to someone and eased to the door. She didn't recognize the other man's voice but distinctly heard him ask about Malcolm being in her office.

"Just doing my check-in. Have you done yours?" she heard Malcolm ask.

Lauren's eyes widened. But then, she had contact with all the players, so it would be expected that Malcolm checked in with her. Had someone seen something? She racked her brain for any improprieties, but they had been careful about their public dealings. She couldn't mess up, not now. But she didn't want to lose Malcolm, either.

Chapter 12

Malcolm and Omar drove to the bookstore after practice. The Grays believed in supporting family and Omar's held a similar principle, so both men had no problems being in attendance. Morgan had dropped Omar off at practice, and they would meet up and drive home together after the signing.

"How are things progressing with you and Lauren?"

"I don't know."

"Ah…okay. What don't you know? You either want her or you don't."

Malcolm sighed in frustration. "I want her. I just don't want to want her as much as I do."

Omar's laughter filled the car's interior. "If that was the case, you shouldn't have touched her."

He slanted Omar a look. "What are you talking about?"

"You know exactly what I'm talking about. And don't bother denying it."

"I had only planned to…we weren't supposed to…hell,

I don't know. One moment we're kissing, the next we're in my bed. The thing that scares me the most is that I'm setting myself up for her to do the same thing again."

Omar shook his head. "Who says she's going to do the same thing? Did she give you any hints that she's thinking of bailing?"

"No. She said she's not choosing the job over me." Malcolm related the conversation he and Lauren had had.

"Sounds to me like you're the one on the fence, not her."

"I'm not on the fence." He wasn't anywhere near the fence, not when he was the one who'd set the pieces in place. He'd jumped clear over the thing like a professional hurdler. He'd known where they'd end up after that card game—intense, passionate sex. He just hadn't counted on the emotional pull he would feel.

"Things didn't go as planned, I take it."

"No. It was supposed to be just sex."

"And it wasn't." It was more statement than question. "You and Lauren have history, and from what Morgan told me, you were planning to marry her."

"Morgan talks too damn much," Malcolm muttered.

"That's the same thing she says about you. With that kind of history, I'm not surprised by the emotional connection. You dated her for two years and were practically engaged. Strong feelings like that can easily be rekindled under the right circumstances, and maybe these are the right ones."

He didn't know if the timing was right or not, but somehow his emotions didn't care. Malcolm hadn't been able to stop thinking about Lauren, and that kiss in her office yesterday had done nothing to satisfy the craving he had developed for her. The feelings he now experienced seemed deeper and more intense. "How do I make it stop?"

"Sorry, bro, but there's no cure. Believe me, I tried. The only thing you can do is surrender and pray things work out this time."

"We'll see."

The signing had already begun when they arrived, and he and Omar took up a position in the back. Lexia looked quite comfortable reading from the book in front of a group of about fifty people. Of course, Malcolm's family had shown up in force to support her. He spotted Lexia's parents, her staff from the café she owned and a good number from the college-age crowd. He tuned back in as she shared a recipe from the book and took questions from the audience.

She ended the signing by providing a sample of the recipe she had shared. Malcolm finally made his way to the front, where she sat signing books. "Congratulations, sis." He kissed her cheek.

Lexia threw her arms around him. "Oh, I'm so glad you made it. How's training camp going?"

"Grueling," he answered with a smile, handing her his copy of the book to sign.

She passed the book back. "You're coming by the house afterward, right?"

"I'll be there."

"Good."

Malcolm went to greet his parents. "Hey, Mom, Dad." He kissed his mother's cheek and shook his father's hand.

"How are you, son?" his father asked.

"A little tired, but good."

His mother patted his cheek. "Make sure you get some rest tonight. Are you planning to stop by Khalil and Lexia's afterward?"

"For a while." He glanced around at the mass of people still surrounding Lexia. "If she ever gets out of here," he said with a chuckle.

"I know. Isn't it fabulous?"

"It is. I'm going to talk to the Gray clan. I'll see you at the house." Malcolm spoke to Lexia's parents and sought out his siblings. They all stood with their spouses, and the possessive hold each man had on his wife was a stark reminder that he was the last single one standing, something that hadn't bothered him in the past.

As always, Morgan hugged him first. "Hey, big brother."

"How are you feeling?"

"Good." She took his hand and, smiling, placed it on her belly.

Malcolm had no words to describe the emotions that grabbed him when he felt the baby move. The little girl he had been attached to at the hip from birth had grown up and would become a mother soon. "He's an active little one."

Omar slung an arm around Morgan and cradled her belly. "He definitely is, especially at night."

Justin and Siobhan laughed, and Siobhan said, *"For real."*

Malcolm glanced Brandon and Faith's way.

Brandon held up his hand. "We don't know anything about that. I get good sleep every night. Well, maybe not every night..." He smiled at his wife.

Faith elbowed him. "Brandon!"

"What? Everybody here knows what we're doing at night, and they're doing it, too."

Morgan shook her head. "I see he still has that speaking-without-thinking thing."

"He's getting better, but I do have to remind him about it every now and again," Faith said, rubbing Brandon's arm.

Brandon placed his hand over his heart, as if wounded. "Hey."

"I said you were getting better."

They all laughed and launched into a discussion of one another's spouses' missteps. A pang of jealousy hit Malcolm, and he immediately shook it off. *What the hell is wrong with me?*

He scanned the room and noticed Khalil stood not too far from Lexia with an expression of pride Malcolm had never seen, even during Khalil's modeling days, when he had received several accolades. An image of Lauren standing in front of a room with her book floated across Malcolm's mind. Would he be standing by her side? Would their relationship even last that long?

Omar had said Malcolm should surrender and pray things worked out. But to Malcolm, that was akin to playing Russian roulette with his heart, and he had no intentions of coming away with it blown to pieces again. The best thing for him would be to step back for a while, but he couldn't see that happening any time soon. Just the opposite—he was as anxious for Tuesday to come as a kid waiting for Christmas.

Lauren sat cross-legged on her bed, so engrossed in her typing it took a moment to hear her cell ringing. She hit the save button and snatched up the phone. "Hey, Malcolm."

"Hey. Did I catch you at a bad time?"

"Nope. Just typing. I can use a break. How was the signing?"

"It turned out well. She had a full house."

If Lauren ever got her book published, she hoped to have the same success. "That's wonderful. Do you know whether she published the book herself or had a publisher?"

"I have no idea, but I can ask. She'd probably be happy to talk to you. Do you want me to give her your number?"

Lauren didn't know if that would be a good idea. If she and Malcolm broke up, would his sister-in-law still talk to her, or would things become awkward? "Um…not yet. I'll let you know when I'm ready."

"Fair enough. That kiss in your office Friday wasn't nearly enough."

She paused at the abrupt change in topic. "Oh? So what would have been enough?"

"Nothing, until I heard you scream my name. And the next time we're together, I'm going to make you scream loud enough to be heard back in Phoenix."

She gasped.

"I'm going to kiss every part of your body, starting at your eyelids, and work my way down to your nose and your cheeks. I'll spend some time at that little spot on your neck right below your ear, using my tongue, branding you. You remember that spot, don't you, sweetheart? As I recall, it's a sensitive area. Do you think if I stayed there long enough, it would produce a kissgasm?"

Lauren couldn't answer. She closed her eyes as her nipples tightened and her pulse spiked.

"I think your breasts will be my next stop. They fit so perfectly in my hands. Mmm… I can feel them now as I massage and rub my thumbs over your nipples. Can you feel me touching you, baby?"

She could more than feel it. "Malcolm," she whispered, her hand going to her belly.

"What, sunshine? You want more? Okay, I'll give you more. What about when I take them into my mouth? I love how hard they get when I suck and circle my tongue all around them."

Her breathing increased, and she slid down on the bed, her body on fire.

"I can't forget how you squirm when I trail my tongue down your belly and to your sweet center. I want to make you wet for me."

No problems there. She was more than wet, and the throbbing in her core increased. She squeezed her thighs together and clenched her teeth. "I'm—"

"Not yet. You can't come yet. Not until I taste you. One long stroke, a short one, another long one… I don't want to miss one drop of that honey."

Lauren couldn't take it. She came in a rush of pleasure that left her shaking. A deep moan escaped her, and she gripped the phone tighter.

"I see your kissgasm and raise you a *phone*gasm. Sleep well and I'll see you on Tuesday, sweetheart."

She dropped the phone on the bed and lay there panting,

still trying to catch her breath. "I can't believe he made me come by talking on the phone." She'd just had *phone sex*! The man was *good*. Clearly some things had changed about Malcolm, and she speculated on how many other women had he done that with. She told herself it didn't matter— they'd been apart for eight years and of course he'd dated other women—but right now she had a hard time convincing herself. Things like this made it difficult for her to keep things moving slowly between them. If she were being honest with herself, Lauren would have to admit that she was falling for him all over again…and hard.

When her body finally calmed, she dragged herself off the bed and ran a bubble bath. She stepped in, rested her head against the edge and closed her eyes. She and Malcolm had only been officially dating less than a month, and she'd already slept with him and tonight…tonight… Just the memory sent her arousal through the roof again. A part of her wanted to call him back and do the same thing to him, but she knew he'd already gone to bed. A smile curved her lips. He wanted to play games? Fine. Come Tuesday, she'd give him a taste—pun intended—of his own medicine.

After her bath, Lauren went back to working on her book, but she had a hard time concentrating. Flashes of that erotic phone call kept intruding on her progress. She gave up forty-five minutes later, powered off the laptop and went to bed.

Lauren woke up the next morning determined to get some work done. She pushed thoughts of her sexy lover out of her mind and, after a breakfast of two boiled eggs and yogurt, settled in with her laptop and starting typing. She spread several books and articles across the table to reference. She also had her graduate thesis, which offered a direct link to the impact of eating habits on performance.

She typed and made notes until her fingers cramped, then reread what she'd written. She made a few changes and, satisfied, decided to pay a visit to her parents.

"Lauren, what a surprise." Her mother engulfed her in a hug and moved aside for Lauren to enter. "Why didn't you tell me you were coming by? We would've waited for you to eat dinner."

"You didn't need to wait." On Sundays, her parents tended to eat dinner around three o'clock, instead of their normal weekday time of six. "Where's Daddy?"

"He's in the family room reading some article on optometry." Her father had worked as an optometrist for almost thirty years, fifteen in his own practice.

"Well, I'll wait to say hello. I know how he gets when he's reading." Lauren smiled. "And I bet you were reading up on the latest in MRI technology, huh?"

"Well, with all these young folks coming in, I have to stay up on what's happening to make sure I have job security."

"Mama, you know they aren't going to replace you. No one can make someone feel at ease going into that little tube as well as you can." She followed her mother to the kitchen and sat at the table.

Her mother took the seat next to Lauren and waved her off. "You're just biased because I'm your mama."

"No, I'm not. I've seen you in action, remember?" Her high school had participated in the Take Your Daughter to Work program, and Lauren had seen firsthand how comforting her mother could be with a frightened patient.

"Enough about that. What brings you by?"

"Nothing really. I just wanted to see you."

"I see."

Her mother's penetrating stare almost made Lauren squirm in her chair.

"Are you sure it's not related to you and Malcolm?"

Why are mothers so perceptive? "Maybe," she mumbled and slumped in the chair.

"I take it the two of you are back together."

"How did you know?"

"It was clear as glass the last time you were here. I figured you'd share when you were ready."

"Things are going so fast, and I'm scared the same thing is going happen again."

"Lauren, sweetheart," her mother said, grasping Lauren's hand, "you can't move forward if you're holding on to the past. As for things moving quickly, I'm not surprised. You and Malcolm were very close in college and I'd venture to say that a lot of those feelings are still there."

Lauren had acknowledged that she still cared about Malcolm the moment she locked eyes with him her first day on the job, but her emotions had taken on a life of their own and she had no idea how to control them. "But what about my job?"

"What about it? Malcolm playing for the team has no bearing on you doing your job. Are there any rules against you dating a player?"

"No."

"Then just take it one day at a time. Honestly, I thought you two would be married by now and I'd have a couple of grandchildren."

Her shocked expression met her mother's amused one.

"I don't know why you're so surprised. I think Malcolm is a very special young man. He always treated you with the utmost respect, and that made him a keeper in my book."

"Gee, thanks, Mom," she said with a chuckle. "That makes me feel even worse." She'd always known her mother liked Malcolm, but her mother had never mentioned anything about the whole marriage-and-kids thing. "You may have liked him, but I'm not too sure about Daddy."

Her mother laughed. "Honey, your father felt the same way. And he was looking forward to season tickets to whatever pro football team picked Malcolm up."

Lauren burst out laughing. "Are you serious?"

"I thought I heard your voice in here," her father said, entering and kissing Lauren's temple.

"Hi, Daddy."

Her father placed his hands on her shoulders. "Job still going well?"

"It's going better than I hoped."

"And how's Malcolm?"

She felt her cheeks warm. "He's fine."

He peered into her face. "That good, huh? Maybe this time I'll get those tickets."

Lauren spun around. "Daddy!"

"I told you," her mother said.

"What? You know that's my team. Well, unless *you* can get me some good tickets."

She shook her head. "I don't think so."

"Well, I need you to put in a good word with Malcolm then."

Her mother stood. "You want some dinner, Lauren?"

"Yes. It's much safer than this conversation." She took in her parents' pleased expressions, and her anxiety over the relationship jumped up a notch. They would be devastated if the relationship didn't work out. And so would she.

Chapter 13

Tuesday, Malcolm had originally planned to hang out with Lauren at his place, but after that phone call on Saturday, felt it best they stayed far away from either of their homes. He had no idea what had possessed him to engage in phone sex with her. He'd never in his life done that with another woman. As a result, he'd been grumpy and horny for the past three nights. She was becoming a distraction he couldn't afford, and he didn't know how to deal with it.

In the past, he'd just tell the woman he needed some distance to focus on the game, and they hadn't balked. For those who complained about the lack of time he had for them during the season, he'd swiftly ended the relationships. But he didn't want to end his relationship with Lauren. And when she opened the door to him wearing another one of those sexy sundresses and a smile that made his heart skip, he knew making any kind of decision would be that much harder.

"Hey."

He kissed her. "How'd the day go?"

"It went okay. Did you sleep in today?"

"Nope. I rarely sleep in these days." And he'd been up at the crack of dawn for the past three mornings taking a cold shower. "Hazard of the job, I guess." He led her to his car and drove them to the marina, where they had dinner before taking a walk.

"I think you have a couple of fans over there," Lauren said, gesturing with her head to two teen boys staring their way.

Malcolm called out a hello and the teens took that to mean they could approach. He shook hands, answered questions and took pictures with them but made sure none included Lauren. After a few minutes, the excited guys ran off, and he and Lauren continued their walk.

"That was nice of you to stop."

He shrugged. "I don't mind. You never know what you might say that could affect someone's life. I remember when I was young and my dad took my brothers and me to a basketball game. I saw one of my favorite players and wanted an autograph. Not only did he refuse, he rudely shoved me aside. I was crushed. It changed my perception of him, and I vowed that no matter what job I had, I would always treat people with respect."

Lauren reached up and kissed his cheek. "And that's one of the reasons I like you."

He liked her, too. A lot. "Come on, let's head down near the water." He waited while she took off her sandals then reached for her hand, lacing their fingers together. Closer to the water, he sat and pulled her down onto his lap. The level of comfort he experienced with her didn't surprise him. It had always been that way. They also didn't need to fill every second with conversation and were content to just sit quietly and enjoy the gentle waves and setting sun.

Malcolm wanted to kiss her badly but held himself in check. Neither of them needed a photo of her across his lap and his mouth planted on hers hitting the front page of some newspaper. Just being out this way was risk enough.

At length, Lauren asked, "Would you be willing to give me a quote for my book when I'm done? After you've read it, of course."

"I'd be honored. How long do you think it'll take for you to write it?"

"I don't know. Some days the information flows well, others…not so much. Hopefully, no more than six to nine months."

Six to nine months meant she expected them to still be dating. Malcolm hadn't had a relationship that lasted longer than six months in the past six years. He'd gotten used to his solitary life and didn't know how to be with one woman for an extended time anymore. The two years with Lauren had been his longest relationship. "Let me know when."

"Thanks." She snuggled closer and shivered.

"Cold?"

"A little."

"We can go." They'd seen a good portion of the sunset.

"I forget how fast the temperatures drop in the evening sometimes. Next time, give me some warning so I can be prepared. I love watching sunsets."

Malcolm kissed the top of her head. "I'll remember that." He helped her to her feet, stood and brushed the sand off his shorts. They reversed their course, leisurely strolling to the car.

Once inside the car, Lauren rubbed her hands up and down her arms.

"Do you want me to turn up the heat?"

"No. I'll be fine in a minute. It's already warm in here. When do you leave for the game?"

"Friday," he answered, merging onto the road. She'd given him the perfect opening to ask for distance, but he couldn't do it. He sighed inwardly. He turned up the music and heard Lauren humming quietly to the latest Jill Scott song. He smiled. "You can go ahead and sing. I know you want to."

She returned his smile. "You know I love singing in the car. And the sound system in my new car is so good, I can blast my music and sing at the top of my lungs."

Malcolm laughed. Flashbacks of her singing with her hands raised in the air popped in his head. "It's a good thing you have a decent voice, otherwise…"

Lauren snapped her head around, and her mouth dropped open. She punched him in the shoulder. "I beg your pardon. I'll have you know I sang in the church junior choir and my high school chamber choir, which was audition only." She pointed a finger his way. "My voice is *better* than decent."

He merely smiled. *That's my girl.* He'd always loved her confidence and take-no-prisoners attitude. He was certain it played a large role in her landing the dietitian position with the team. While there were a few women filling the role for other teams, her gender and age might have made a less self-assured person think twice about applying.

When they got to her house, Malcolm hesitated getting out, not ready to end the evening on one hand and contemplating running away forever on the other.

He walked her to the door.

"I enjoyed myself tonight, Malcolm," Lauren said, looping her arms around his neck.

"So did I." So much so that he wanted to back her into the house and bury himself deep inside her. But he settled for kissing her with a hunger that astounded him. He had to leave. Now. He'd gotten in too deep, too fast. "The next few weeks are going to be pretty intense and I need to stay focused, so—"

She cut him a look and slowly removed her arms. "So you need some space."

"Yes. No…" He sighed deeply. "That's not what I'm trying to say. It's just…" He didn't know what he was trying to say, but his words and his heart were running toward opposite ends of the field.

"I get it. No problem," she said curtly. "You still don't really trust me, do you?"

"I never said I didn't trust you. Don't put words in my mouth." How she had seen into that small corner of his heart that still harbored the hurt of the past, he didn't know.

Lauren scrutinized him a long moment.

"I trust you." As much as he could for the time being.

"You probably should get going. I don't want to be responsible for you missing curfew." She stepped through the door. "Good night, Malcolm."

"Lauren…" She folded her arms, hurt and confusion lining her features. He'd already stuck his foot into his mouth once and decided he should leave well enough alone for tonight. "Good night." She closed the door softly, and Malcolm felt as if she'd closed the door on them.

He loped back down the walk to his car. His mind said he'd done the right thing—they needed to slow down—but his heart said just the opposite.

Lauren spent Wednesday and Thursday compiling all the body compositions and weights of the players, along with the goals from the coaches, and sending them to the players with her recommended dietary changes. The information would also be sent to management by the end of the day. There were a few players who had gained weight, and she wondered how that would affect their status on the field.

She didn't have to wonder long, because Thursday afternoon one of the players burst into her office, angry about his numbers.

"You just cost me my position!"

Inside Lauren was shaking like a leaf, but she refused to let him intimidate her. "I don't know what you're talking about, Carlos. I have nothing to do with who does or doesn't play." Carlos Jenkins, an offensive lineman, stood six eight, weighed 280 pounds and had dark, piercing eyes and a handsome coffee-with-cream face that was contorted with anger.

"You're the one who's going to tell Coach I'm over my weight limit by eight pounds."

"All I do is report the information. I sent it to you with a few recommended changes that would get you back to your goal weight pretty quickly." Because of all the physical activity, it didn't take football players long to drop the pounds, whereas most other people would struggle for weeks.

"I know you haven't sent the information to the coaches yet, so I need you to change those numbers."

Lauren stared at him incredulously. "Excuse me? You're asking me to lie?"

"No, I'm asking you to keep my secret, and I'll keep yours."

What secret? The hairs on the back of her neck stood up. His was the voice she'd heard talking to Malcolm outside her office that day. "So, blackmail. I'm sorry, Carlos, but I will not alter any numbers."

Carlos braced his hands on her desk and leaned down. He smiled coldly. "You sure about that? I wonder what management would say if they found out their new dietitian is knocking boots with the star running back."

Her heart nearly stopped. She and Malcolm had been very careful while at the office. "I'm not sure what you're getting at."

"I saw Malcolm Gray leaving your office last Friday pretty late. And the door was closed…" He let the sentence hang.

Lauren slowly pushed to her feet. "Two other players were in my office right before that, *with the door closed*. Are you accusing me of sleeping with them, too?"

"I know what I saw. Like I said, you do this one thing and no one has to know."

She met his glare with one of her own. "Then do what you think you need to do, because I'm not changing those numbers." They engaged in a stare down, and Lauren didn't flinch.

Carlos threw her one more hostile stare, let out an animalistic growl and stormed out, slamming the door.

Lauren collapsed in her chair and dropped her head in her trembling hands. She couldn't decide which emotion had the upper hand at the moment—fear or anger. She voted for anger. She jumped up and paced the office. The man must be out of his mind to try to blackmail her. No way would she mess up the best job she'd ever had over some stupid threat. Not like she needed to, anyway. She stopped pacing and sighed heavily. Malcolm wanted space…or *something*. So she'd give it to him. He still didn't trust her. He said he'd let go of the past, but clearly he still held on to some things. As much as it pained her, she had to. She just wished she could shut off her feelings in the process.

Right now, she had to determine what to do about Carlos. Should she go directly to Mr. Green and let him know about the confrontation or let it go? Lauren didn't want to be that tattletale who always ran to tell the teacher, but she also didn't want anything to come back on her. She paused with her hand on the doorknob. No, she'd wait to see how things played out. Whatever the coaches decided had no bearing on her job.

Rounding her desk, she finished the rest of the reports, sent them to the respective coaches and packed up to leave. Since the team would be gone tomorrow, she really didn't need to be on-site, so she planned to work from home in her pajamas.

Lauren opened the door, glanced over her shoulder and surveyed her desk and conference table one last time to make sure she had everything. She hit the light switch, turned back and ran into a solid mass. She let out a small squeal and jerked away, almost losing her balance.

Strong hands banded around her waist to steady her. "You okay?"

She clutched her chest. "Malcolm, you scared me half to death." Ignoring how being in his arms made her feel, she asked, "What are you doing here?" She took a deep breath and released it gradually, trying to slow her runaway heartbeat.

"I wanted to see you."

Her gaze darted up and down the hall, and she moved out of his embrace, praying no one had seen them. She already had one person threatening her and didn't want to give anyone else something to talk about. "Why? I thought you wanted some space."

Malcolm reached for her again, and she pushed his hand away. He sighed. "Those were your words, not mine."

"But it amounts to the same thing. I have to go. Have a safe flight tomorrow and good luck with the game." Lauren tried to move around him, but he blocked the doorway.

"Can I just have five minutes, please?"

"No. We don't want to give anyone else something to talk—" She cut herself off and wanted to slap a hand over her big mouth. *Great! Just great.*

He frowned. "What the hell does that mean? Did someone say something?"

She waved him off. "Nothing. I'll see you later." She pushed past him and rushed down the hallway. She didn't stop until she got to her car. Her cell phone rang as soon as she closed the door. Seeing Malcolm's name on the display, she tossed it on the seat next to her and let it go to voice mail. If she gave him those five minutes, one look in his eyes and he'd have her weak and agreeing to any and everything he had to offer.

Instead of going straight home, Lauren took a detour and went shopping. A little retail therapy would improve her mood.

An hour later, Lauren emerged from the Del Amo

Fashion Center with a deep-blue bra and matching pair of panties from Victoria's Secret's Dream Angels Wicked collection, aromatherapy body wash from Bath & Body Works, two milk-chocolate truffles from Godiva, and a new tube of her favorite MAC Oh Baby lip gloss. The golden-bronze color worked well for casual or dressy. She'd also picked up a Santa Fe salad from BJ's Restaurant and Brewhouse.

When she arrived home, she unloaded her haul and curled up on the sofa to eat her dinner. She turned on the television and surfed until she found a rerun of *Major Crimes*. Of course it had to be the episode focusing on the relationship between Detective Sykes and Lieutenant Cooper, bringing to mind her own relationship woes.

Maybe she should have listened to Malcolm's explanation, but she was afraid to put herself all the way out there again. Her growing feelings were stronger than before and, truthfully, they frightened her. She refused to settle for a one-sided relationship similar to the one she'd had in Phoenix, where she gave everything and he gave whenever it happened to be convenient. Putting Malcolm out of her mind, she focused her attention on the show and her food.

Later, Lauren ran a bath and added some of the foam bath she'd just purchased, deciding on the stress relief fragrance. While the tub filled with the scent of eucalyptus and mint, she checked the messages on her phone. She read a text from Valencia lamenting about an issue at work. "Join the club." She sent a reply detailing what happened with Carlos. One minute later, her phone rang. "I knew you would call," she said with a laugh.

"Girl, did you report his behind?" Valencia asked.

"No. I sent the report to the coaches, and now the only thing I can do is wait to see what he does. Now, you said you're still covering for the new dietitian?" She turned off the water.

Valencia's heavy sigh came through the line. "This

woman was hired less than three months ago, but she's always got some issue as to why she has to be off. First, it was her back. Next, it was her wrist and now her hip. And she takes off three or four days each time."

"I can't see them keeping her on much longer if she keeps this up."

"Me, either. But I wish they'd decide one way or another, because this is wearing on the rest of us. Now back to you. Did you tell Malcolm?"

Lauren didn't answer.

"You didn't, did you?"

"I don't want him interfering in my job, just like he wouldn't want me to with his." She could imagine Malcolm's reaction and didn't want to cause him any trouble.

"I get that, but what if this guy outs you two? Malcolm doesn't deserve to be blindsided."

She flopped back on the sofa. "I hadn't thought of that. But I know Malcolm. He'd march right up to the guy, and all hell would break loose. I'll think about it, though. Anyway, girl, my bubble bath is getting cold. I'll call you tomorrow."

"Okay. Keep me posted."

"I will, and you do the same. Talk to you later." Lauren disconnected and noticed she had a voice mail from Malcolm. She hesitated briefly, not sure she wanted to hear what he had to say. But curiosity propelled her to dial the number and listen.

"Lauren, I know you think I don't want to see you, but that's not the case. I also know that I'm taking a risk of losing my man card by telling you this, but honestly, this thing between us seems to be moving at a pace that scares the hell out of me. So, yeah, though I feel like I need some space, I want you in my life more. I'm not giving you up. I'll talk to you when I get back, sweetheart. Oh, and I haven't forgotten about that comment."

Lauren held the phone against her heart. She was fighting a losing battle. And, somehow, she didn't care.

Chapter 14

Malcolm missed a second pass during the walkthrough Friday morning. He cursed under his breath. He'd never been this distracted, and he attributed it to Lauren, but not in the way he'd originally considered. In the past few weeks that he'd been seeing her, never once had he had difficulty putting thoughts of her aside while on the field. Now, with things unsettled, he couldn't stop thinking about her and, as a result, had dropped two easy passes he should have been able to catch with his eyes closed.

Marcus passed him. "You okay, Malcolm?"

"Yeah, fine," he gritted out. Frustrated and angry with himself, he took a deep breath, recentered and went out for the next play. Thankfully, his focus held for the next hour and he didn't embarrass himself further.

Afterward, the team showered, went through the TSA check set up at the practice facility—something that teams had started to make the flight process quicker—and then rode the bus to the airport for their trip to Houston. He lay back against the seat and stared out the window as the rest of the team and staff boarded. They used the same chartered plane from a national airline chain and the same flight crew every time. The layout offered each player the equivalent of one and a half seats, with first class reserved for the bigger linemen. Malcolm turned on his cell and was disappointed to find that Lauren hadn't responded to his message. He was honest enough to admit that he did have some lingering trust issues, but he felt they could overcome them with time. Had she decided not to give them a chance? If she had, he planned to do everything in his power to change her mind. His finger hovered over the call button for a few seconds, wanting to hear her voice and clear the air, before he decided against it. He'd told her what he wanted her to know for now. The rest could wait until he saw her.

"Thinking about your situation?"

He rotated his head in Omar's direction. "Is it that obvious?"

Sitting across the aisle, Omar stretched out one long leg. "About as obvious as it was when you missed those two passes earlier."

Malcolm chuckled wryly. "Sounds like your game in the season opener two years ago." At the time, Omar and Morgan had been going through a rough patch in their relationship, and Omar's concentration had taken a nosedive.

"That was the worst week of my life. My suggestion is you get whatever it is straightened out before the regular season starts."

He appreciated Omar not using Lauren's name. Anyone who might be listening wouldn't know what the conversation entailed. "Yeah, I know." It also brought to mind the question of how long he and Lauren would have to hide, and he decided that would be another topic for them to discuss.

Malcolm put the phone in airplane mode, closed his eyes and made himself comfortable for the three-and-a-half-hour trip. Unlike on normal flights, lunch consisted of a three-course meal that fell in line with the players' dietary needs, as outlined by Lauren.

After landing, they traveled by bus to the hotel. To minimize public contact, several measures had been put in place—separate entrances, key-controlled elevators, private floors and a dedicated security staff. Not even employees were exempt. They couldn't ask for autographs and pictures or post on social media without consequences. All of which ensured players were rested and left undisturbed. Malcolm dropped his bag on the chair in the hotel room that would be the first of many for the season and stretched out on the bed. His veteran status afforded him a room to himself, but players in their first or second years had to double up. A quick glance at the nightstand clock showed the time to be just after five, which left him two hours to rest before dinner. He would have preferred to order room service, however, team rules prohibited its use, along with accessing the room's minibar or going to the hotel's bar.

He had just dozed off when his cell buzzed in his pocket. Groaning, he fished it out and checked the display, then smiled and sat up. Siobhan had sent him photos and videos of the transitional housing's grand opening, and he immediately saw her PR skills at work. Malcolm's heart swelled at the video of a single mother and her two children seeing their home for the first time. The two girls, who looked to be between six and eight, ran from room to room, their happy squeals filling the air, while their mother dropped to her knees and said a prayer of thanksgiving. It made him take stock of how blessed he was, and he vowed to always do what he could to help others.

Malcolm clicked on the final message and smiled at the attachment. Instead of replying, he activated his video messaging and called.

"Hey, baby brother," Siobhan said when she answered.

"Hey, sis. Thanks for sending the pics. Looks like everything went well."

"Oh my goodness, Malcolm. It was *awesome*! I've cried so much today, they sent out a memo saying the drought in California is over."

Malcolm laughed. Though his sister's eyes were slightly red, they were also sparkling with joy. "Congratulations, mama. I thought you guys had another week or so before Christian came to stay permanently."

"I have no idea what happened. All I know is Justin and I got a call while we were at the opening from his social worker saying we could take him home."

"And I bet you were there before she could complete the call."

"Just about," she said with a laugh. "You should see Nyla. She's been following him around since we got home. And Christian is just as happy about being a big brother. We're going to have dinner here Sunday afternoon, sort of a welcome party. I know you and Omar will be getting in late tomorrow, but I hope you guys can pop in for a few minutes."

"Tired or not, you know I'll be there. Where is he?" Siobhan walked into a bedroom, and he heard laughter and his niece's happy giggles.

"Here they are. Christian and Nyla, Uncle Malcolm is on the phone." She turned the phone so he could see the children.

"Hey, Christian. How's your new room? Hey, Nyla."

Christian's face lit up. "It's good." He turned around and tried to point out everything in the room. "And see my bed? It has *PAW Patrol* on it."

Malcolm had no idea who or what a *PAW Patrol* was, but he nodded. "That's pretty cool. Well, I'll see you in a couple of days, okay?"

"'Bye." And he was gone.

Siobhan laughed. "So, I guess the conversation is over."

She held the phone toward Nyla. "Say hi to Uncle Malcolm."

He waved. "Hey, Nyla. How's my baby girl?"

Nyla babbled something, tried to eat the phone, then got upset when Siobhan wrestled it out of her hands.

"That's it for the phone, little girl. Here's your book." That seemed to satisfy her. Siobhan came back to the phone. "I see you're all reclined on your bed. Are you in for the night?"

Malcolm yawned. "Nope. Dinner is in an hour, then we have a chapel service and pregame meeting."

"Oh. Okay. How are things with you and Lauren?"

Malcolm had figured that with everything going on, his sister would have forgotten about his love life, but he should have known better.

He obviously hesitated too long, because she said, "What did you do?"

He told her about him wanting space. "I didn't say those words exactly, but in Lauren's mind, it meant the same thing."

"You're afraid history's going to repeat itself. I totally get that, Malcolm, because I did the same thing with Justin... more than once. Thank goodness my husband is a patient man." She chuckled. "Otherwise I might have missed out on the best thing that has ever happened to me. Stop fighting your feelings for Lauren. Take it from me—all it does is make things worse."

"I don't recall asking for any advice. Don't you have enough to worry about?"

Siobhan rolled her eyes. "Like that's going to stop me from giving it. And I'll never have so much to worry about that I can't be there for you. Remember I changed your stinky diapers. That gives me privileges."

Malcolm laughed. "Really, Vonnie? Why are you bringing up old stuff? It's definitely time for this conversation to end."

She blew him a kiss. "Love you. Be careful tomorrow, and have a safe trip home."

"Love you, too. I will, although I probably won't play more than a few downs."

Justin appeared in the picture with Christian on his shoulders and Nyla in his arms. "What's up, Malcolm?"

"Hey, Justin. I see you're busy."

"Yeah, but I'm loving it." His smile matched Siobhan's. "Later, bro."

"All right. Gotta go. See you Sunday."

"'Bye, sis." Malcolm disconnected, his smile still in place. He tossed the phone on the bed and resumed his position. He adjusted the pillow under his head and stared up at the ceiling, thinking about his sister's unsolicited advice. He'd never imagined having feelings for Lauren again and didn't know how to stop fighting against the fear that had a grip on his heart. But one thing Siobhan had said rang true. He felt worse now than he had three days ago.

Lauren pulled the grocery cart up the steps leading to her condo and into the house. Valencia had teased her about looking like an old lady, but Lauren didn't care. She could carry all her bags in one trip instead of two or three. And today she had more than usual. She'd put off shopping last week and had to replenish just about everything, including the basics like flour, salt, eggs and milk. It took her longer than necessary to unload because she was hungry and kept stopping to snack.

She put everything away, except for the items she planned to use for cooking. Lauren usually spent her Sundays doing meal prep for the week. With it being summer, she opted for light menus that included salads with shrimp or chicken and one-dish dinners—combined vegetables, meat and occasionally pasta—that took less than thirty minutes to prepare. She started with the shrimp and made enough to include in a shrimp-avocado salad and to sauté with asparagus. It would have been much easier to make or grab a sandwich daily, but Lauren tried hard to stay away from eating too much bread, so she learned to be creative with her meals. Bread topped the list of her most favorite foods and she had, once or twice, inhaled an entire loaf of warm French bread covered in butter over the course of one night.

Lauren removed the shrimp from the pan and added a small amount of butter and the asparagus. She cooked it just until it was tender and spooned it onto a plate to cool. Just as she lined up the bowls on the counter, her doorbell rang. She hoped it wasn't her new neighbor who had moved in earlier in the week. The woman had come over three times asking to borrow first a screwdriver and a hammer, then later, after returning the tools, she'd asked if Lauren had a blanket she could have because she'd misplaced hers in the move and didn't feel like going shopping for one. Lauren had been so outdone that it took her a moment to respond. Using all the home training her parents had raised her with, she told the woman she didn't have a spare one.

She snatched open the door, ready to say no to whatever the woman wanted but went still upon seeing Malcolm.

"Hey, baby."

It took her a moment to find her voice. She hadn't returned his call or replied to his voice mail. "Um…hey. Come on in. I'm in the kitchen."

Malcolm followed her inside and closed the door. "Smells good. Is this for the week?"

She divided shrimp and asparagus into two containers. "Pretty much. I just do enough to take care of a few days, in case I don't feel like cooking when I get home." He watched her silently for a few moments. "I didn't expect to see you, with you just getting back and all."

"I know, but you didn't call me back and I wanted to make sure we were clear on a few things."

"I didn't call you back because you needed to be focused for your game," she said, not looking in his direction.

Malcolm gently turned her to face him. "You didn't call me back because you were upset," he countered. He pulled her into his arms. "I meant what I said, Lauren. I'm not giving you up. Not without a fight. That first day you showed up at the training facility, I was angry and hurt all over again, and I never thought we'd be here. I'm still scared as hell that we'll end up like before, but I can't stop what I'm feeling. And I think you're feeling the same thing."

His intense gaze dared her to lie. "I am, and I'm just as afraid as you are, Malcolm." Truthfully, she'd fallen in love with him all over again, but now wasn't the appropriate time to tell him. What if he didn't feel the same? The chemistry between them had always been strong, and she could see him reacting to it and viewing their connection as nothing more than lust. Lauren stepped away and continued putting away her food.

He leaned against the counter and folded his arms. "So what do you want to do about it?"

She gathered her haul and placed it in the refrigerator. "We could continue as we are…if that's what you want to do." She moved the dirty dishes to the sink to wash later, wiped down the counters and hazarded a glance his way.

Malcolm angled his head and studied her. "Yeah. But that's not all I want."

Her pulse spiked. "What do you mean?"

"Are you done in here?"

"Yes. I'll wash up everything later."

Malcolm reached for her hand, led her into the living room and gestured her to the sofa. "For starters," he said, sitting next to her, "I think we need to slow things down. Not sure how that's going to work out, since all I want to do every time is see you is strip you naked and make you scream."

Lauren blinked.

"But as you pointed out that night on the dance floor, we've both changed, and I want us to take time to get to know each other all over again."

She hadn't expected him to say that. "I think that's a good idea. So, that means no more kissing and…"

He cut her a look. "Oh, I didn't say all that. I will be kissing you just as soon as we're done with this conversation. As far as the sex, we'll see how it goes."

"But you just said…"

"Yes," he said slowly. "But I'm also a man who's very attracted to you and who remembers with vivid clarity how it feels to be inside you." He shrugged. "I'll do my best, but that's all I can promise. Hell, I'm having a hard time resisting carrying you to your bed right now."

Lauren's body came alive with his declaration, and it took all she had not to drag him there herself.

Malcolm placed a soft kiss on her lips. "Lucky for you, I can't stay long. Otherwise…"

She smiled as a wicked thought crossed her mind. "You did say we would still kiss, right?"

"Yes."

"And if I kissed you right now, you wouldn't resist?"

"Hell, no."

"That's all I needed to know." She pushed him down on the sofa and straddled him.

Malcolm's eyes widened. "Lauren, what are you doing?"

"I'm going to kiss you, that's all." Lauren just hadn't said where. She leaned down and kissed him with a thoroughness that had him groaning. She slid down and moved her hands under his shirt, taking it higher and higher as she kissed her way from his rock-hard abs to his well-defined chest and back down again.

"You're going to get yourself in trouble," he said through clenched teeth.

She silenced him with another kiss and continued her journey down his body. She grasped the waistband of his basketball shorts and rid him of them and his briefs. He tried to sit up and shift his body, but she held tight.

"Baby, no!" He cursed and jerked upright as she took him into her mouth.

But she didn't stop. And she didn't plan to until he screamed *her* name. His stomach muscles contracted beneath her hands and his legs shook. She swirled her tongue from base to tip and sucked him in deep, eliciting another guttural moan. He'd taught her how to please him, and she wanted to show him that she remembered every lesson and had picked up a few tricks on her own.

"Lauren, baby," he panted, gripping the back of her head and keeping her in place. She increased the pace, and he went rigid and exploded. *"Lauren!"*

Lauren didn't stop until the last spasm left his body. She lifted her head. He lay sprawled with his eyes closed, hands fisted and his breathing ragged. "Should I take that to mean you're liking my kisses a little more now?"

Malcolm opened his eyes but made no comment.

She sat back, a satisfied grin covering her mouth. "I see your phonegasm…"

He chuckled. "Girl, you ain't nothing nice."

"That's not what you were screaming a minute ago."

He sat up and braced his hands on his thighs. "I thought we agreed to go slow."

She smiled serenely. "We can go as slow as you like now. Oh, and your man card is safe with me."

He shook his head. "I need to clean up."

"I'll get you a towel." While he cleaned up in the half bath, Lauren did the same in her master bathroom and met him back in the living room.

"Do you have any plans for the rest of the afternoon?"

"Not really. Why?"

"Wanna take a ride with me?"

"Sure." She glanced down at her shorts and sleeveless blouse. "Do I need to change?"

"Nope," he said with a smile. "You're fine."

"Where are we going?"

"You'll see."

Lauren eyed him for a lengthy minute and went to get her shoes and purse. Half an hour later, he drove them into an upscale residential area and stopped at a house that had several cars parked in the circular driveway and in front of it. "Whose house is this?"

"Justin and Siobhan's."

She went still. "Malcolm, I don't think this is a good idea." She knew how Morgan felt about her and could imagine what the rest of the family thought.

"I think it is. If you hadn't interrupted our conversation, I would have told you the rest."

"What rest?"

"That we're done hiding our relationship."

"We can't… I mean…what if—" Her head was spinning. Carlos's threat came back to her.

Malcolm grasped her hand and brought it to his lips. "Sweetheart, there are no rules against us dating. I don't plan to go all out when we're at work, but I'm not going to avoid you or not say anything when our paths cross. As far as my family, they already know."

Lauren rubbed her temples and groaned. "Your family hates me. I can't go in there."

"My family does not hate you."

She skewered him with a look. "Morgan?"

"She'll be fine." He got out, came around to her side and extended his hand. "It'll be okay. I promise."

She sighed and placed her hand in his. If this didn't go well—and she didn't see how it could—she would never speak to him again.

Chapter 15

Lauren let Malcolm lead her up the walkway to a large house with a meticulously manicured lawn. She expected him to ring the doorbell, but he just opened the unlocked door and gestured her in. "Shouldn't you ring the bell or something? We can't just walk in," she whispered.

"Whenever we get together, we always leave the door unlocked. Go on in."

As soon as she crossed the threshold, she heard laughter coming from somewhere in the back. Her gaze was drawn to the glossy natural maple hardwood floor. As followed the sounds, she surveyed the house's open layout, with each room flowing seamlessly into the next one. Her steps slowed as they reached what she figured was the family room. When they noticed her and Malcolm, every eye turned their way and all laughter stopped abruptly.

Malcolm shook his head. "Hey. You all remember Lauren."

His mother seemed to recover from shock first and

rushed over. "Hello, Lauren. It's so good to see you again."
She gave her a warm hug.

His father followed suit.

"Hi, Mr. and Mrs. Gray. It's nice to see you, too."

"Congratulations on your new job. That's quite a feat.
We're going to bring these men into the twenty-first cen-
tury yet," Mrs. Gray added with a wink.

Lauren smiled, feeling slightly better. "Thank you."
While everyone else wore shorts and tees or tanks with
flip-flops or sneakers, Mrs. Gray had on a pair of navy
slacks and a navy-and-white printed short-sleeved blouse
with dressy two-inch heeled sandals. Her face looked as if it
had been expertly made up and not a strand of her cropped
salt-and-pepper layers was out of place.

"Welcome to our home, Lauren," Siobhan said, embrac-
ing her. "This is my husband, Justin, our daughter, Nyla,
and the newest member of our family and the reason for
this celebration, Christian."

Lauren smiled at the little girl and boy staring her way.
The fact that Christian was older than Nyla and had been
referred to as the newest member had her thinking that
they'd adopted him. "Hi, Siobhan. They're adorable." She
didn't remember Siobhan being so open and relaxed and
wondered if it had to do with the handsome man at her side
and her children.

Justin placed a kiss on her cheek. "Nice to finally meet
you, Lauren. I've heard a lot about you."

Lauren glanced at Malcolm over her shoulder. What had he
told his family? "Same here. You guys have a lovely home."

"Thank you," he said. "Make yourself comfortable."

She noted the curious gazes of two women she had
yet to meet, but guessed they were Brandon and Khalil's
wives. They came toward her with smiles, introducing
themselves—Faith was married to Brandon and Lexia to
Khalil—then steered Lauren over to where they had been
seated. Brandon and Khalil greeted Lauren with hugs.

"What's up, Lauren?" Omar asked.

"Hey, Omar."

He glared at Morgan, and she reluctantly mumbled a greeting.

Trying to remain friendly, Lauren asked, "When's your baby due?"

"Next month."

"Congratulations. I hope all goes well."

"Thank you."

Omar kissed Morgan on her temple and smiled. "Thanks, Lauren."

She made small talk with Lexia and Faith and found out that Lexia owned a café and Faith was the vice president of the Grays' home safety company and worked as a website designer. Both women suggested they meet for lunch sometime, but Lauren didn't commit because she had no idea how her relationship with Malcolm would play out. Still weighing heavily on her mind was the bombshell he'd dropped about them going public.

After playing with his niece and nephew, Malcolm finally made his way to where she sat and handed her a bottle of green tea. "See, I told you it would be okay."

Lauren accepted the bottle, mumbled a thank-you and rolled her eyes.

"What?" he asked with a little laugh.

"You should've warned me…and them that you were bringing me."

Malcolm regarded her thoughtfully. "You're right. I'm sorry."

She met his sincere gaze. "Why didn't you tell me?"

"Because I didn't think you'd come, and I really wanted you here." He ran a gentle finger down her cheek and kissed her.

Why is he doing this? she wailed inwardly. Before she could question him further, Khalil came over.

"Okay, you lovebirds. Y'all save all that for later."

Lauren felt her face warm.

Malcolm snorted. "I know you're not talking, as many times as I caught you and Lex—"

Lexia jumped up. "It's time to eat. I'm going to start setting everything out." She grabbed Khalil's hand. "Come help me."

"And make sure that's *all* you two are doing," Malcolm called out.

Khalil turned back and smiled. "No promises." He tossed Lauren a bold wink and followed his wife into the kitchen.

For the first time, she saw that he wore a hearing aid and vowed to ask Malcolm about it later.

Once the food had been laid out, everyone gathered around and held hands while Mr. Gray blessed the food and offered a prayer of thanksgiving for Christian coming into their lives. After a rousing *amen*, everyone filled their plates and sat around eating and talking.

Lauren watched the men interact with their wives and felt a twinge of envy. Anyone would be able to see the love flowing between the couples. She tried to concentrate on her food and not worry about the possibility of her and Malcolm never having the same thing.

"What's on your mind, sweetheart?" Malcolm whispered.

"Nothing. Your brothers really love their wives."

He scanned the room. "Yeah, they do. But none of them had an easy path to get to this point. They put in the work, and even though they messed up a few times, they stuck it out."

Did that mean he wanted the same for them, and were his feelings deeper than he'd let on? She really wanted to find out, but this wasn't the time or place. When she finished, Lauren rose to take her empty plate to the trash. Morgan was in the kitchen, and Lauren braced herself for a confrontation.

"I don't want you to hurt my brother again."

She sighed. "Morgan, I don't plan to hurt your brother. I didn't plan to the last time, either, but youth and listening to friends caused me to lose a good man."

Surprise lit Morgan's eyes. "What do you mean?"

"Let's just say I was already insecure, and all it took was hearing a couple of horror stories from my friends who'd dated athletes. Don't tell me you've never made a mistake before."

"Yeah, I have." She paused as if remembering. "How do you feel about my brother?"

"I love Malcolm. I don't think I never stopped," she said wryly.

"Have you told him?"

"No, and please don't say anything."

Morgan folded her arms and narrowed her eyes. "You don't want me to say anything to him, yet you're admitting it to me. Why?"

"Because you're the only one who's convinced I have ulterior motives…and I don't." Lauren held Morgan's gaze unflinchingly.

"Morgan, Lauren…what's going on? Morgan, you aren't…" Malcolm divided a wary gaze between them.

Morgan waved him off. "We're fine. Stop worrying." She rounded the bar and kissed his cheek. Giving Lauren a nod, she departed.

"Are you sure nothing happened?" he asked, searching Lauren's face.

"Positive." She grabbed his hand and dragged him back into the family room. She only hoped he hadn't heard any of her conversation with Morgan. Especially the part about her loving him.

Malcolm kept an eye on Lauren for the rest of the afternoon. He didn't believe for one minute that nothing had transpired between her and Morgan. His twin had made it clear on several occasions how she felt about Lauren, and he didn't think she had changed her mind overnight. But he was pleased by how the rest of his family treated her. He hadn't intended to ask her to accompany him because, in his mother's eyes, it would be tantamount to an announcement of permanency, but he'd wanted her with him. Maybe the thought of being the only single person had prompted the invitation. As Lauren had pointed out, it was hard to miss the love between all the couples, and today, for reasons he couldn't explain, he didn't want to be the odd man out.

He studied Lauren as she talked to Faith. She took a sip from her water bottle and licked her lips. The sight instantly conjured up images of that little impromptu session at her house earlier. His groin stirred, and Malcolm tried to shift his thoughts to something else, otherwise every person in the room would get an eyeful. He couldn't believe what she'd done. And that little thing she did—sucking him deep into her mouth while her tongue made circles around his shaft—always drove him out of his mind. He had no idea how she did it, but no other woman had come close to making him feel the way she did.

Brandon came to where Malcolm stood. "Those must be some thoughts, baby bro."

"I don't know what you're talking about."

"Sure you do. It's the same look I have when I want to make love to my wife. Just ask Khalil, Omar or Justin. They know. Seems like your feelings for Lauren are a little stronger than what you want us to believe."

Malcolm eyed him. "What makes you think that?"

Brandon chuckled. "The fact that you brought her to a *family* gathering, for one. And, for another, your emotions are all over your face. Better hope Mom hasn't seen it." He started humming the wedding march quietly.

A wave of panic hit him, and he searched out his mother.

He relaxed upon seeing her playing with her grandchildren. He met Brandon's smug gaze and wanted to punch him.

Still chuckling, Brandon clapped him on the shoulder. "Let me know if you want to talk about it. I'll be more than happy to help you out with this thing called love. Although, since you've been there before with Lauren…"

Malcolm shrugged Brandon's hand off. "Get the hell away from me." He refused to acknowledge the truth in his brother's statement. He wasn't in love. Yes, he liked Lauren. Yes, he wanted to be with her, but that didn't mean he was in love with her. His heart started pounding in his chest, and the panic came back. He had to get out. He went through the kitchen and stood out on the deck, waiting for his heart to get back to a normal pace. He wasn't supposed to fall in love with her this fast. They had agreed to go slow, and this would complicate everything.

He heard the sliding door open and turned. "Hey, Dad."

His father stepped out and closed the door. "Everything okay?"

"Yes, I'm fine."

"You sure you're not running scared because you just realized you love Lauren?"

Malcolm couldn't very well tell his father the same thing he'd said to Brandon—not and live to tell about it—so he kept his mouth shut.

"Son, we've all been down the road you're on, and though it seems frightening sometimes, being able to find that special one to share your life with is worth it all. When I first realized I loved your mother, I was running so fast, I could've broken Usain Bolt's record in the one hundred."

He met his father's smile. "I never thought about that. You and Mom seem to always be in sync."

"Oh, we are…now. I almost let her get away with my foolishness." He shook his head and chuckled. "I want you to remember something. We men are quick to run off, but we come back just as quickly. A woman hangs in there for a long time deciding what to do, but once she decides to leave, she's gone for good. Don't ever let her get to that point if you love her."

Malcolm stared out into the yard, processing his father's words. The thought of Lauren closing the door on them for good made his stomach churn. "Thanks, Dad."

"Any time, Malcolm. Now, let's go get some of this cake Lexia made."

Inside, Siobhan was helping Christian cut pieces of cake and pass them out. Lexia had done the *PAW Patrol* theme—Malcolm still had no idea who or what that was. By the looks of the cake, he assumed it had to be some comic or book character and made a mental note to ask Siobhan about it.

"Is everything okay?"

He slid an arm around Lauren's waist. "Yeah, baby. Everything's good." When she smiled up at him, it took all his control not to blurt out that he loved her. He promised they'd go slow, and he would try to stick to that agreement, even if it killed him.

After the cake, Christian opened the mound of presents his new family had bought, from clothes and room decorations to puzzles and a motorized car. Malcolm and Omar had purchased football jerseys in the Cobras team colors of purple and silver—a white one with the accent colors for home and purple with silver for away—with his first name on the back and a football, also with Christian's name on it.

By the time the family gathered to leave, Christian had fallen asleep in the middle of the floor with the football tucked under one arm and a puzzle under the other. Nyla had lost the battle to sleep an hour ago. Malcolm stood off to the side observing his family saying goodbye to Lauren. He saw her exchange numbers with Faith and Lexia and hug Siobhan and his mother. Though Morgan didn't offer any type of affection, she did say goodbye, and that gave him hope. If Malcolm could leave the past behind, so could Morgan.

Once they made it to the car, Lauren let out a long breath and leaned back against the headrest. "You're lucky it didn't turn out bad, because if it had, I was never speaking to you again." She rolled her head in his direction. "After I punched your lights out."

Malcolm threw his head back and roared with laughter. When he finally calmed down, he drove off and said, "That's a serious punishment, baby. But I was never in any danger."

"Why's that?"

"I know my family. And I knew they'd treat you just like they always have. Well, except Morgan."

"Yep. Except Morgan."

"I know you said nothing went down between you two in the kitchen, but somehow I don't believe that."

She didn't reply for a moment. "She just warned me not to hurt you again. I told her I didn't plan to. After that, it was fine."

He still didn't believe her, knowing his sister, and he intended to call Morgan later.

"I noticed that Khalil has a hearing aid. I don't remember him having one."

"There was a gas explosion across the street from the building where my family's company is located, and Khalil just happened to be outside talking on the phone. A few people were killed and several others injured. Khalil was thrown several feet, had broken ribs and a sprained wrist and lost his hearing for several weeks." The memory of that time rose to the surface, and he thanked God every day that his brother hadn't been one of the casualties. "If it wasn't for Lexia, I don't think he would have made it through the ordeal. He'd basically shut all of us out."

"Oh my goodness. He was fortunate."

"Very. He regained full hearing in one ear after almost

two months and had surgery to repair the eardrum on the other. He only has about fifty percent hearing in that ear."

"Wow. Lexia is very nice, but I thought she owned a café. You said she helped him?"

He laughed. "Her café is on the first floor of the building, and she was there with him until help arrived. Brandon talked her into visiting him in the hospital. Khalil wouldn't eat, yelled at any of us if we tried to help in any way...he was in a bad place. But he loves Lexia's low-fat coffee cake, so she brought a piece. I wish I'd seen it, but apparently when he said he couldn't eat, she told him his hand was fine—and so was his mouth with all the yelling and fussing she could hear out in the hallway—handed him a fork and said 'eat.'"

Lauren burst out laughing. "She seems so sweet and quiet. I can't imagine her doing something like that."

"Ha! Don't let that little pint size fool you. She doesn't take any mess. Neither does Faith, for that matter. They fit right in with my sisters." And so did Lauren. She didn't hesitate getting into his face during their confrontations.

"Sounds like they do." Silence rose between them. "When we left, you mentioned not hiding our relationship anymore. You meant just around your family, right?"

"No. Like I told you earlier, there's nothing that says we can't date and I'm not going to jeopardize your job in any way, but I'm not going to avoid you or barely say two words when I do see you. And if I want to walk you to your car when you leave when I'm not practicing or in a meeting, then I want to be able to do that. There's nothing to worry about, sweetheart."

"I'm not so sure about that," she mumbled.

Malcolm frowned, recalling her comment in her office on Thursday. "Wait. Has somebody said something? When I came to talk to you last week, you said mentioned not giving someone something else to talk about. What did you mean?" She didn't respond. His eyes left the road briefly and he saw her tight features. "Talk to me, Lauren."

"It's nothing."

"If it's nothing, then you can tell me about it. Do I need to pull over so we can talk?"

"No," Lauren answered quickly.

"Then let's hear it."

"First you have to promise me you won't say anything or do anything."

"Why do I need to—"

"Promise me, Malcolm."

He blew out a long breath. "Fine. I promise."

"Well, one of your teammates gained a few pounds, and you know how I send out the weight and testing results with any suggestions to the players and the coaches?"

"Yeah. I like that. It helps us stay on track."

"Which is why I implemented it. But the guy who came in accused me of costing him his starting position and asked me to change his weight before sending the information to the coach. Then he said…"

"Said what?" he prompted when she didn't continue.

"He said he'd keep my secret if I made the change."

"What secret?"

"Us."

Malcolm whipped his head in her direction. *"What?"*

"Eyes on the road, Malcolm."

He jerked back into his lane. He didn't understand. They'd been very careful in their dealings. "What did he see?"

"Nothing. He just said he saw you leaving my office late one afternoon and the door had been closed. I told him that two other players had been in my office right before and asked if he was accusing me of sleeping with them, too. That was after I refused to change those numbers."

Malcolm clenched his teeth and bit back the acerbic comment poised on the tip of his tongue. He never should have made that promise. "Who was it?"

"I'm not going to say. He got my message loud and clear. I just didn't want you to be blindsided if he told other players and they asked you about it."

"Then it's even better that we're going public. It won't matter who he tells." He still wanted to know who had tried to blackmail her, but he understood she wouldn't say. "Still worried about it?" he asked, trying hard to keep the anger out of his voice.

"A little, I guess."

"You don't need to. If he does anything to hurt you, he'll answer to me."

"Malcolm, you promised you wouldn't do anything."

"I know." But promise or no promise, if the coward got in her face again—teammate or not—he would find out how Malcolm felt about him threatening Lauren.

Chapter 16

Every time someone knocked on her office door Monday, Lauren jumped and her stomach lurched, thinking it was Carlos. Or worse, Malcolm coming to camp out just in case. By lunchtime her nerves were shot, and she decided to eat outside on one of the benches on the walking path. She found one positioned beneath a shade tree and hurried over. For the time being, she didn't have to worry about Carlos since practice didn't end for another hour.

While eating her shrimp and avocado salad, she thought about her time with Malcolm's family. Aside from the tension between her and Morgan, everyone else had been as nice as she remembered. His parents seemed to still be very much in love, and she'd noticed them sharing a kiss or an intimate touch on more than one occasion. The same could be said for all the couples in attendance, and she found herself feeling a little envy. She and Malcolm were progressing, but Lauren longed for the relaxed contentment she had seen on all their faces.

Although he hadn't said so, she knew he still didn't trust her completely. Not that she blamed him. But it made her speculate on whether the relationship would crumble with the slightest test. If she could go back in time, she would definitely do things differently, starting with not listening to her friend back in college. She and Malcolm still might have broken up eventually, but it wouldn't have been because of her.

Lauren forked up another portion of the salad and realized how much she liked it. She'd found the recipe on the internet while looking for some lighter summer dishes. Thinking about recipes reminded her that Nigel had asked her to stop by. She finished her lunch, drained the green tea and headed back to her office to drop off the containers and pick up the large gift bag.

She found Nigel seated on a stool at the back of the kitchen making a list. She placed the bag on the counter next to her.

He glanced up at her entry. "Hey, Lauren."

"Hi, Nigel. It always smells so good in here." She didn't know what he and his staff were cooking for lunch, but it made her mouth water, despite the fact that she'd just eaten.

Nigel smiled. "You're welcome to grab a plate. We cook for the staff, too."

"Maybe next time. I just ate. You said you wanted to see me."

"Yes. I'm making the grocery list and I remember you mentioning a couple of new snack recipes you wanted to try."

"Oh, yes. I've had several of the guys—mostly the rookies and first-year players—complain about having to cut back on their sweets, so I wanted to try out a couple of lower-fat and low-sugar treats."

"What did you have in mind?"

Lauren pulled out her phone and clicked on her memos where she had noted the recipes. "One is a brownie recipe that uses dates and dark chocolate and doesn't need to be baked. It's just over one hundred calories per serving and has less than four grams of sugar."

"Anything without sugar *can't* be labeled a dessert," he teased. "Hey, that's the number one requirement for me."

She laughed. "True, but since we have this regimen to consider…" She shrugged.

Nigel waved a hand. "Yeah, yeah. What else you got?"

"The other one is an apple-peach crisp." She passed him her phone so he could see the recipe. "It's about two hundred fifty calories, and we can even add a little light ice cream on top."

He shook his head. "No butter, no sugar. This is just sacrilegious, Lauren."

Lauren burst out laughing. She pointed to a line on the recipe. "There's honey."

He slanted her a glance. "Three tablespoons…in the crumb topping." Still shaking his head, Nigel said, "Okay, but if I get any complaints, I'm throwing you under the bus."

"Whatever."

He chuckled. "I'm just giving you a hard time. These sound really good." He checked several cabinets. "I have most of the ingredients. Just need to get the fruit." He wrote the items on his list. "Anything else you want to try?"

"Actually, I made some cookies."

He gestured toward the bag. "Is that what you have in the bag?"

"Yep." She had found a recipe that called for a small amount of coconut sugar, dark chocolate chips and peanut butter. Thankfully, no one on the roster had a peanut allergy. She dug out a Ziploc bag and opened it. "Here, try one."

Nigel took one, bit into it and chewed thoughtfully. "I hate to admit it, but these are good. I hope you have enough."

"I hope so, too." Lauren had made several dozen cookies that were about three and a half or four inches in diameter. "I'll leave them here and you can add them to the buffet. How are the morning recovery shakes working out?"

"Very well. My staff has taken to making a few extra because the coaches seem to enjoy them."

The news made Lauren smile. Having the coaching staff buy in to her recipes and suggestions meant the possibility of longevity in the position. A couple of staff members passed her with large bowls filled with fruit and salad mix. "Glad to hear it. I'll get out of your way." The team would be descending on the dining room shortly, and she wanted to be gone so as not to run into Carlos or Malcolm.

"I'll probably try out the brownies tomorrow. Feel free to pop in."

Now that her plan had been implemented, Lauren didn't really need to be in the dining room during meals too often. She stopped in briefly a couple times a week just to answer questions or check on her more problem athletes. But she did want to find out how well the new dessert was received. "I may do that."

Nigel picked up the bag. "Thanks, Lauren."

With a wave, she departed. She made it halfway down the hall before she heard male voices. *Great.* Several guys passed her and spoke. She returned their greetings but didn't break stride.

"It's too bad you didn't take my offer."

The soft, menacing voice stopped her. She met Carlos's dark, cold eyes. She quickly scanned the hallway, praying Malcolm was nowhere in sight. However, since Carlos, like most of the players, loomed over her like a mountain, she couldn't see anything. Carlos stood waiting for her to respond, but rather than get into a confrontation, she chose to ignore him. Lauren turned away from his glare only to lock eyes with Malcolm.

"I need to talk to you for a minute."

"Malcolm—"

Malcolm leaned closer and said for her ears only, "If you

don't want me to pick you up and carry you out of here, then you should start walking."

Not wanting to cause a scene, she said, "Sure, I have a couple of minutes." He followed her to her office and closed the door. Lauren rounded on him. "I thought you said you weren't going to go all out and…and…whatever." She threw up her hands.

He folded his arms. "I didn't. I only said I wanted to talk to you. If I were going all out, I would've kissed you like I did when we were playing gin."

She stared.

"What? No comeback?" He laughed softly.

No, she didn't have a comeback. "You said you wanted to talk to me."

"What did Carlos say to you?" He held up a hand. "I saw your expression, Lauren, and I know he said something to upset you."

"It was nothing I can't handle." She went over to her desk and straightened a stack of folders.

Malcolm came around the desk and rotated her to face him. "He's the one who threatened you, isn't he?"

She opened her mouth to lie, but the scowl on his face stopped her. "Yes," she said resignedly.

He released her and stalked toward the door muttering, "When I get done with him…"

Lauren rushed around the desk, stepped into his path and blocked the door. "*No!* You promised me you wouldn't say anything to him."

"The man is three times your size, Lauren," Malcolm snapped. "I'm not going to stand by and let him bully you."

She placed her hands on his chest. "Malcolm, please don't. I don't want you to get into trouble, and I already handled it."

His jaw tightened. "That doesn't mean he won't try to do something to hurt you. I will *not* allow that to happen. Don't fight me on this, baby."

Sheryl Lister   169

She would never forgive herself if Malcolm got suspended or worse, fired, and had to get him to see reason. "Listen to me. He's not going to hurt me. He can't. If no one knew about us before, they do now. You didn't leave much room for question whispering in my ear," she added wryly. "Baby, I couldn't take it if you ruined your career for me. This is my job and I won't let him or anyone else bully me into doing something wrong or illegal. You have to let me deal with it my way."

He let out a frustrated breath, brought his hands up to frame her face and rested his forehead against hers. "You're killing me, baby. All I want to do is protect you."

Her heart skipped. She loved this man. "If I need you, I'll let you know. I promise."

Malcolm kissed her softly and nodded. "I need to go shower."

She wrinkled her nose. "Yes, you do."

He smiled for the first time. "You're a cold woman."

"No, I'm a truthful one."

He gazed down at her. "I... I'm glad you're back in my life, Lauren." He gave her one more kiss that nearly melted her to the floor and slipped out.

Lauren leaned against the closed door and smiled. Maybe they would make it this time.

Omar slid into the chair across from Malcolm in the dining room. "So, that's the new definition of discreet?"

Malcolm glanced up from his plate. "I told her yesterday we weren't hiding anymore."

"Feel better now?" he teased.

He smiled. "Shut up." He didn't know if *better* was the right word. Their time together would be limited now that the season was in full swing. The schedule didn't allow another weekend off until two months from now, when the team had a bye week. They typically had a day off during the week, usually Tuesdays when the regular season started, but Lauren didn't have the same schedule. And Malcolm typically still came in for a short workout. That only left the evening, and those two or three hours wouldn't be nearly enough to satisfy him.

Marcus set his plate on the table, went back for something to drink and came back. He leveled Malcolm with a stare. "So, what's up with you and Lauren?"

Omar chuckled and kept eating.

"We're dating."

"Ah, moving kind of fast, aren't you? You just met the woman. She's only been here, what, two months or so?"

He cut a piece of his chicken and ate it before responding. "I didn't just meet her."

"Malcolm and Lauren go way back," Omar tossed out nonchalantly.

Marcus divided a questioning glance between Malcolm and Omar. "Like how far back?"

"College," Malcolm said. "We dated for almost two years."

"Well, I'll be damned. I know a couple of players whose feelings are going to be hurt," he said with a laugh, gesturing across the room.

Malcolm turned in the direction Marcus indicated and saw Lauren smiling and talking to Darren. For a split second, he felt a surge of jealousy. Then he calmed down. This was her job. She had to talk to the players. He shrugged. "Not my problem. She's mine."

"So, what happened the first time?"

Malcolm didn't like rehashing the story, but he relented. "A couple of my buddies went to a party, and one of them got drunk. The other one called me and asked me to come help get him back to the dorm." Malcolm had lived off campus, but his friends had known he'd be studying at the library that night for a kinesiology exam. He told how he went to the party, searched for his friend and convinced him to call it a night. "We got him outside and two girls followed, trying to persuade us to stay. Both had had a little too much to drink." He paused as the painful memory came back. "Lauren and her roommate happened to be passing just as the girl plastered herself all over me and tried to kiss me."

Marcus shook his head. "No need to say more. I hope it works out this time."

So did Malcolm. He finished eating and stood to leave. The running backs' meeting wouldn't start for another twenty minutes, but he had something he needed to do first. "I need to go talk to Coach for a few minutes." Both men looked at him with concern. Knowing he could confide in them, Malcolm braced his hands on the table and quietly told them what Carlos had done.

"So do we kick his ass now or later?" Omar asked.

Marcus made a move to stand.

"I promised Lauren I wouldn't say anything to him, but I never said I wouldn't mention it to the coach or management," Malcolm said.

Slow grins spread across Marcus and Omar's faces, and Marcus said, "Okay, but if he threatens her again, all bets are off. I'll leave Jaedon to pick up Carlos's remains." His attorney brother was ruthless in the courtroom and had been instrumental in taking down Omar's former agent, who had tried to ruin Omar and Morgan's reputations.

Malcolm nodded. "We think alike. I'll see you later." He passed Carlos on the way out, and it took a great deal of control to keep that promise he'd made.

He knocked on Coach Smith's open door. Martin Smith had been head coach of the Cobras since the beginning of Malcolm's career, had taken the team to the playoffs seven of those eight years and brought home the championship trophy three times. He reminded Malcolm of retired coach Tony Dungy because of his uncanny way of connecting with the players and his calm demeanor. The two even favored one another slightly, with the exception of Coach Smith's darker skin. "Hey, Coach. You have a minute?"

Coach Smith waved Malcolm in. "Sure, Malcolm." He set aside his papers and clasped his hands together on the desk. "What can I do for you?"

He reached for the door. "You mind if I close this?"

"Not at all." He frowned. "Is everything all right? You're not coming in here to tell me you're retiring?"

Malcolm smiled. "I still have a couple good years left in me, so I'm not retiring yet."

Relief flooded the other man's face. "Thank goodness."

"I wanted you to hear it from me first that Lauren Emerson and I are dating."

His eyebrows shot up. "Really?"

"Yes. She and I have…history. I assure you this won't affect either of our jobs."

"Well, there aren't any policies against it, so I'm not following why you needed to make an announcement."

"There's something else." He paused a beat. "She's been threatened by one of the players who wasn't happy about her reporting his weight stats."

Coach leaned forward, concerned. "Exactly what do you mean by threatened…physically?"

"No." Malcolm shared the details of the threat. "He wanted her to do the same thing Stan did last year."

Coach scrubbed a hand down his face and rose to his feet. "I thought we handled all of that."

Malcolm wondered if Carlos had been part of the original scheme and had somehow slipped through the cracks. It could be why the man had felt bold enough to approach Lauren the way he had.

"Who is it?"

"Jenkins."

"Carlos?"

"Yes."

Coach Smith shook his head. "I'll talk to Green."

"I'd appreciate it if you didn't mention me talking to you to Lauren."

A smile broke out on his face. "Don't want her to know you're interfering in her business."

"No." If Lauren found out, she'd be livid. Malcolm's feelings for her now were stronger than they'd been in college, and he couldn't risk losing her again.

He clapped Malcolm on the shoulder. "You don't have to worry about her finding out."

"Thanks, Coach." Malcolm left feeling much better. If management dealt with Carlos, he wouldn't have to.

Malcolm didn't get home until after eight. He was tired but wanted to talk to Lauren. He trudged up the stairs to his bedroom, tossed his keys on the dresser and removed his shoes and shirt. He stretched out on his bed and called the number that topped his frequent-caller list.

"Hey, Malcolm," Lauren said when she answered.

"Hey."

"You sound tired. Are you just getting home?"

"Yep. How'd the rest of your day go? You didn't have any more problems, did you?"

"It was fine, and no. You should probably go to bed."

"What? You don't want to talk to me? I think my feelings are hurt."

She laughed. "Silly man, your feelings are fine. I'd love to talk to you all night, but I know how exhausting your day can get."

Malcolm had always appreciated that about her. She never hassled him about the long hours he put into football. "Would you really?"

"Really what?"

"Talk to me all night."

"Yes."

"Then talk to me, baby."

"What do you want to talk about?"

"I don't know. Everything. Nothing." The sound of her

voice seemed to ease the weariness steeped in his bones, and he wondered if this was what his brothers meant by coming home to that special one. "You said you've changed. Tell me what's changed about you."

"Okay. Hmm…let's see. I'm not insecure anymore, and I go after what I want."

Malcolm's heart rate kicked up a notch. What was she telling him?

"But I still like to eat my Baskin-Robbins chocolate-chip ice cream in two cones."

He laughed so hard he started to choke. "I can't believe you still do that." The first time they'd gone to the ice cream shop, she asked for a second cone, and when they got back to his apartment, she'd divided the one scoop between the two cones, saying she liked a little ice cream with her cone. "And you still only get the one scoop?"

"Yes, I do."

"I thought by now you would have at least graduated to two scoops."

"Whatever, Malcolm Gray. I bet you haven't changed much, either."

"And you would be right." He liked keeping his things a certain way, and when he was younger he'd often gotten into fights with Khalil and Brandon because they would always rearrange his books or his collection of miniature cars just to get a rise out of him.

"Do you still have your Hot Wheels?"

"You'd better believe it."

"I don't recall seeing them when I was there."

"That's because I have them stored in my shed."

"What?" she asked with mock surprise. "I can't believe you just tossed them in a box somewhere."

"You must be out of your mind, woman. I did *not* just toss them in a box. Each one is wrapped and boxed individually and stacked *neatly* in the storage container." Lauren's laughter came through the line. They continued to talk and tease each other, and when he checked the time, over two hours had passed. He had enjoyed their conversation and was reluctant to end it, but tomorrow promised to be another long day with practice, meetings and watching film.

"It's getting late."

"I want to talk to you longer, though."

"Mmm...me, too. I missed talking to you this way, Malcolm."

"I missed this, too, sunshine." He never remembered wanting to spend hours on the phone talking to the women he dated. Lauren was the only one. They'd been friends first, and maybe that made the difference. "But I need to go to bed."

"Can we do this again?"

"Any time you want."

"Sleep well, angel eyes."

Malcolm laughed softly. "'Night, sweetheart." He swung his legs over the bed and plugged the phone into the charger on his nightstand. His thoughts went back to what she'd revealed. *I'm not insecure anymore, and I go after what I want.* Good, because so did he. And he wanted her.

Chapter 17

Lauren stood in the tunnel watching practice. It had been almost three weeks since she and Malcolm had spent time together. While she enjoyed their nightly phone calls, she wanted to feel his lips on hers and run her hands over every inch of his hard body. Training camp had ended two weeks ago, and this Sunday would be the first game of the regular season. Malcolm had asked her to go with him early and wait for him after the game. Her eyes were glued to him as he executed a movement with the power, speed and agility of a cheetah. "Mmm, mmm, mmm...that body," she murmured. And he belonged to her.

There were fewer players on the field, and she learned some had not made the cut. She also didn't see Carlos and wondered if he'd been benched because of his weight gain. She shook her head. Had he followed her suggestions, he would have most likely already lost the excess pounds. Lauren was proud of Darren, however. He had shed every one of his twenty pounds, plus five more, and she looked forward to seeing him in the starting lineup Sunday.

Lauren stood there a moment longer then went back to her office. Two hours later, she looked up and saw Malcolm standing in her doorway.

"Hey, beautiful."

"Hey yourself, handsome. Are you coming to give me one of the hundreds of kisses you owe me?"

Malcolm closed the door and came toward her. "Hundreds?"

"Hundreds," she reiterated.

"Since I only have five minutes, I'd better make it count." He pulled her flush against him and crushed his mouth against hers in a long, drugging kiss. "It feels like it's been forever since we've had time together."

His hands roamed up and down her body as he reclaimed her mouth. She held on as his tongue made sweeping, swirling motions, driving her out of her mind with desire. Lauren's hands found their way under his shirt, and he promptly captured them.

"Don't do that," he said, his breathing as ragged as hers. "I have to go. I'll call you tonight."

She groaned.

"I know. I'll make it up to you. Talk to you later."

Lauren dropped down in her chair and closed her eyes. Her body pulsed everywhere. It was only Wednesday, and she had to wait four days. She had agreed to take things slow, but she didn't know how much more of *slow* she could take. Right now she wanted it hard and fast. Groaning again, she sat up. She still had two more hours to go before her day ended.

As she packed up to leave later, remnants of the kiss played around the edges of her mind. It would only take a minute to stop in the dining room and seek out Malcolm for just one more. *Do not go to the dining room. Keep walking, girl. You're a professional.* She hated that annoying voice in her head, but this time she grudgingly agreed. Her steps slowed as she pushed through the front door and she saw Malcolm leaning against the column. He gently removed her tote from her shoulder and threaded his fingers through hers.

"I decided I wanted to walk you to your car today. Objections?"

Lauren smiled up at him. "Not one." Once they reached her car, he pinned her against the door and gave her a kiss so achingly tender it melted her heart.

"I don't know how much longer I can go without seeing you, Lauren," Malcolm whispered as he trailed kisses along the shell of her ear. "Feel how much I want you."

She felt the solid ridge of his erection pressed into her belly. "I want you, too." She reached down to stroke him, and he shuddered.

He stilled her hand. "You're about two seconds away from me straddling you on this hood and not caring about everybody and their mama seeing me make love to you. Get in your car and go home before you get us both in trouble."

"Oh, I don't know. Right now I might be okay with getting into trouble," she said with a sultry smile, tracing a path from his chest to his abs.

He chuckled. "You were never this forward back then, but I think I like this new, bold you." He held the door open. "This weekend. You and me."

Lauren slid into the driver's seat, and he closed the door. She started the engine, waved and drove off. She glanced in her rearview mirror and saw him drag his hand down his face. *At least I'm not the only one struggling for control.* Between the kiss in her office and this last encounter, he had every molecule in her body screaming for release, and she didn't think she'd make it until the weekend. She couldn't believe she'd been so reckless as to not care whether someone saw them making out in the parking lot. "Good grief," she muttered.

Two hours after she arrived home, Malcolm was still on her mind. He typically called around nine, and for the past couple of nights they had talked until almost midnight. Tonight, Lauren decided to shower first so all she had to do was slide under the covers after their conversation.

Her cell rang as soon as she slipped a short tank sleep shirt on. "Hello."

"Hey, girl," Valencia said.

"Hey, Lyn."

"Did I catch you at a bad time? You sound weird."

"No. I just got out of the shower. I'm fine." Other than needing to release some sexual tension. "How's it going at work?"

"Miss Thang finally got fired, thankfully, and they just hired someone else. I've been home at my regular time for a week and it's glorious."

Lauren laughed. "Good for you. It's about time. I can't believe they took so long to let her go."

"Me, either. Anyway, I called to see how things are going with you and Malcolm. I'm like two weeks overdue for an update. Oh, and whatever happened with that football player who was threatening you? Did you tell Malcolm about him?"

She shook her head. "You want to let me answer one thing at a time?"

"My bad," Valencia said with a little giggle. "Let's start with the football player and save the juicy stuff for last."

"I don't know what I'm going to do with you, girl. Anyway, I have no idea what happened to him. I didn't see him practicing today, so he could have been benched or something. I did tell Malcolm about him, and I had to make him promise to not confront the man."

"Aw, that's so sweet." She let out a whoop. "Go, Malcolm. Protect your woman."

"Yeah, that's what he said."

"That's because he still loves you."

"He hasn't said anything about love." But everything about the way he had been behaving of late reminded her of when he did. Did she dare hope? Her phone beeped with another call. "Hold on, Lyn. That's Malcolm."

"Go talk to your man. Call me tomorrow."

"Okay. 'Night." Lauren switched over. "Hey, sexy."

Malcolm's deep rumble came through the line. "My thoughts exactly. What are you doing?"

"Sitting here wishing you were here."

"Is that right? And if I were?"

A wicked thought crossed her mind. She still owed him for that phone sex call. "If you were here, I'd start with kissing you until I was drunk with your taste. Then I'd strip you naked and take my time skating my tongue across your chest, lingering a bit on each nipple."

"And?" he said, his voice sounding strained.

"Oh, I have to touch you. Mmm… I want to feel your abs quiver beneath my hands as I continue my taste and touch quest. I love your smooth caramel skin, and it tastes as sweet. And your hard, strong thighs…just what I need to hold me up when we… Oh, wait. We're not there yet. I want you to be hard for me. Are you hard yet, Malcolm?" She heard his labored breathing through the line, but he didn't answer. "You have to be so I can take you deep into my mouth, slide you in and out and use my mouth and tongue at the same time…"

Lauren heard a beep and looked at the display. The call had dropped. She smiled and called back, but he didn't answer. She frowned, waited a few minutes and tried again. The call went straight to voice mail. "What the…?"

Why wasn't he answering? Puzzled, she sighed heavily and flopped down on the bed. Playing that little game had her so aroused it wouldn't take much to push her over the edge. She got up to turn on the ceiling fan, needing to cool off. She sprawled across the bed directly under the flow of air and waited for it to take down the blaze. The ringing doorbell startled her. Who would…? Her eyes widened.

Lauren scrambled off the bed, went out front and glanced through the peephole. *Malcolm?* She undid the locks and opened the door. "Malcolm. What are you—" He hauled her into his arms, kicked the door shut and captured her mouth with an urgency that stunned them both. He placed her against the door and drew her legs around his waist.

"Are you trying to send me to prison?" he murmured huskily, pressing hot kisses along her jaw and exposed throat and grinding his erection in subtle circles against her center.

"I…what… I don't know what you mean." She couldn't think, much less talk.

"I broke every speed limit to get to you." He moved her panties to the side and slid a finger inside her. "So wet."

She whimpered, already on the verge of an orgasm.

"I can't wait, baby."

He entered her on one deep thrust, snatching her breath. "Malcolm, we can't…protection?"

"Already in place. You asked me if I'm hard for you. The answer is hell yeah, I am. Can you feel how hard you make me?" he asked, retreating to the tip and pushing back in inch by incredible inch until he was buried to the hilt. "How do you want it, baby?"

"Hard and fast."

A wolfish gleam leaped into his eyes. "Then that's how I'm gonna give it." Malcolm palmed her bottom and held her firmly against the door.

Lauren wrapped her arms around his neck and locked her legs around his broad back as he set a hard, driving rhythm that rattled the door. She arched and writhed against him as he pumped faster, delving deeper with each thrust. He whispered a mixture of tender endearments and erotic promises that made her desire climb even higher. Their breathing grew louder as he gripped her tighter and drove into her harder. The pressure built inside her with an intensity she'd never felt, and she convulsed and screamed his name as waves of ecstasy crashed through her so violently she thought she might pass out.

"Look at me, sweetheart."

She met his gaze, and what she saw took her breath away.

A moment later, he threw his head back and erupted, shouting her name hoarsely. "You're mine, Lauren. I love you, baby."

Lauren collapsed against his shoulder. She didn't know how long they stayed there, gasping for air and shuddering with the aftershocks of their lovemaking.

Her head popped up. "What did you say?"

"I said I love you, Lauren Emerson."

His words brought tears to her eyes. "I love you, too, Malcolm Gray."

A smile curved his lips. He carried her down the hallway to her bedroom and placed her in the center of her bed. He undressed them both, climbed in and gathered her in his embrace.

"What are you doing? Don't you have a curfew?"

"I'm in for the night. They never said I had to sleep at my house," he added with a wink.

Lauren lifted her head and burst out laughing. "Well, I can't say how much *sleep* you're going to get, and I owe you for hanging up on me."

Malcolm rolled on his back. "Then punish me, baby."

She grabbed hold of his growing erection. "With pleasure." She wanted this to be a night he'd never forget and planned to show him how much she loved him. How much she *still* loved him.

Malcolm woke up disoriented for a moment, then remembered. He stared at Lauren cuddled into his side, her head on his chest. He hadn't woken up next to a woman in years, but he wanted to wake up next to her every day for the rest of his life. The admission was freeing in a way. He'd told Lauren he loved her last night, but what he hadn't said was that he had never stopped. All those years he'd thought he'd been over her, but she'd remained somewhere in the dark recesses of his heart, occupying a space that no other woman could ever claim. He leaned up to see the time. Five fifteen. As much as he wanted to lay her on her back and awaken her with his kiss, they both had to work. Fortunately, he didn't have to lift weights this morning, so he had a little leeway.

Carefully shifting Lauren, he eased out of the bed and went into the bathroom to dress. When he came back, she was awake. "Morning, beautiful."

"Good morning," Lauren murmured. "What time is it?"

"Five thirty. I'm going to head out. I'll see you tonight."

She smiled sleepily. "Are you coming over?"

He nodded. "I want to talk to you about something." He kissed her. "Go back to sleep. I'll lock the door."

"Mmm-hmm." She closed her eyes.

Malcolm stepped out into the cool early-morning breeze and walked the short distance to where he'd parked his car. He got in, turned on the headlights to cut the darkness and backed out of the space.

At this early hour, traffic was sparse, and he made it back to his house in under twenty minutes. He tossed the duffel bag on a chair in his room and went to his large walk-in closet. He searched for a minute until he found the box he wanted. Taking a seat on his bed, he took a deep breath. He'd packed the box away eight years ago, and this was the first time he had thought about opening it. He picked up the first item and removed the bubble wrap to reveal a framed photo of him and Lauren that had been taken at the beach. Malcolm laid it aside and reached for the black Camaro Hot Wheels car she'd given him as a reminder to never give up on his dream of owning the real thing. He dug deeper until he found what he was looking for. The small navy velvet box still held the promise ring he'd given her. And that she'd returned. He was ready to make another promise. A promise of forever.

Chapter 18

Despite getting only three hours of sleep, Lauren breezed into work Thursday morning feeling more energized than she had been in a long time. Malcolm's declaration of love still resonated in her heart. After that second round of love-making, he had gone out to his car to bring in the overnight bag he'd packed. Their shower together had turned into another passionate session, with him taking her from behind while she braced her hands on the wall. Her core pulsed with the memory of his slow, hypnotic thrusts.

"Morning, Lauren."

She whipped her head around. "Good morning, Charlotte." She'd been so lost in her fantasy that she hadn't even heard Mr. Green's assistant behind her. Shaking her head to clear it, she unlocked her office, unloaded her tote and powered up her laptop.

Lauren needed to get her mind in work mode. She had check-ins this morning with three of the rookies who'd made the cut, including Brent and Chris. Each would stop in between their morning meetings or workouts. Breakfast ran from six until nine, allowing players, coaches and support staff time to eat at their convenience, depending on their meeting and weight-lifting schedule. Players also had access to the training room, where they could seek information from medical staff or, if injured, receive treatment.

She pulled their files, penned a few notes and set them aside. Rotating in her chair, she checked her email. She read one from Nigel telling her he'd be adding the brownies to the day's menu and asking her to stop by some time that morning. "Now's as good a time as any." On the way, she ran into Darren.

"Hey, Lauren."

"How's it going, Darren?"

Darren grinned. "Great! Did you see my numbers?"

"I did. Congratulations."

"Coach said I'd probably be able to start. I don't know how to thank you."

They spoke to a couple of players as they entered the dining room. "All I did was set the program. You put in all the work, and it shows." The lineman's large frame looked more defined, especially around his midsection.

"You going to be around this afternoon?"

"Yes."

"Can I stop by? There's something I want to show you."

Lauren mentally went through her schedule. She wanted to leave a little early, because she planned to cook dinner for her and Malcolm and she had to pick up a few ingredients. "What time are you free?"

"I can make it between three and three thirty."

"Perfect. I'll see you then."

He gave her arm an affectionate squeeze. "Thanks."

She smiled up at the gentle giant. "You're welcome." When he walked away, she turned and saw Malcolm watching with an unreadable expression. She waved, and he relaxed and smiled. Rather than approach him like she wanted, she reminded herself that she'd see him later and went to speak with Nigel.

Lauren made it back to the office just as Chris showed up and spent the rest of the morning with several other players popping in. She had planned to eat outside, but an impromptu early-afternoon meeting with the coaches left her with fifteen minutes to wolf down her pasta with chicken and asparagus before heading down to one of the smaller conference rooms. When she'd first explained how she wanted to collaborate with them on each player's needs and goals, they'd seemed excited by the idea and wasted no time implementing it. She wanted to build a program for the long haul.

Darren came by as promised a little after three. He had a smile so bright, Lauren asked, "What are you so happy about? I mean, besides reclaiming your starting position."

Darren came and stood in front of her. "My girlfriend said I'm marriage material now and I'm going to ask her to marry me."

"Oh my goodness! That's wonderful." Without thinking, she reached up to hug him.

He returned the hug. "I can't tell you how much I appreciate everything you've done. Look." He took out a small ring box. "Do you think she'll like it?"

Lauren brought her hands to her mouth. "Wow. It's absolutely beautiful." A row of smaller diamonds surrounded a round-cut solitaire that had to be at least two carats. "I know she's going to love it. Congratulations."

"Well, isn't this cozy?"

She and Darren turned to see Malcolm standing in the doorway, his eyes cold.

Darren divided a glance between them, then asked Lauren, "You and Gray?"

She nodded tightly.

"Thanks again, Lauren. I'll let you two talk." He beat a hasty exit.

Malcolm didn't waste any time. "So I guess you were looking for a bigger ring."

"I beg your pardon?"

"Don't try to play me, Lauren. I know what I saw."

Lauren put a hand on her hip. Was he insinuating she had something going on with Darren? "Do you?"

"The hug, the ring, the smiles, the way he was touching you in the dining room the other day… I just don't know what to think." He pivoted and started to walk out.

She stormed across the room and got in his face. "Are you *kidding* me? You think that I could tell you I love you one day and be with another man the next?" She shook her head wearily. "After everything you've said, you still don't trust me, do you?" She wasn't going to bother explaining her conversation with Darren, because Malcolm should know better.

"It's kind of hard to when I walk in and see my woman hugging another man holding a ring in his hand. You're going to tell me I'm wrong?"

"No. I'm not going to tell you anything. You should know me."

He didn't comment.

Angry tears burned her eyes. "See, you won't even deny it. This isn't going to work, Malcolm."

"Then tell me I'm wrong," he said through clenched teeth. He reached out for her, and she pushed him away.

"I shouldn't have to!" Lauren should have left well enough alone—friendship and nothing more—because it was now clear to her that he'd never let go of the past. "After everything we've been through, I can't believe you'd think I'd turn around and cheat on you, especially with someone you work with. You need to leave my office." She stepped around him and kept her back to him.

"Lauren, I—"

She turned and held up a hand. "Just go. I guess that

makes us even now. I broke your heart, and now you've broken mine."

Something like regret flickered across Malcolm's features, and he reached for her again.

She shook her head, trying to keep the tears from falling. His jaw tightened, but he did as she asked.

Once he was gone, she closed the door and let the tears flow. She didn't have any other appointments, so she sent an email asking Mr. Green if she could leave early to take care of some things. He replied favorably, and she was packed and striding down the hall a moment later.

"Lauren, are you okay?" Omar asked as she exited the building, gently taking hold of her arm.

If she opened her mouth to say one thing, the floodgates would open, and she couldn't do that here.

"Malcolm?"

Lauren nodded.

He seemed to understand and gave her a reassuring hug. "It'll all turn out okay. Just hang in there."

She really wanted to believe him, but her world had just gone to hell in a handbasket in a matter of seconds. She couldn't see anything past the pain in her heart.

Malcolm paused in pacing the locker room when Omar entered wearing a deep scowl on his face. "What's wrong? Is Morgan okay?"

"What the hell did you do to Lauren? I just met her damn near running out of the building and crying."

His heart constricted. "I walked in on her and Darren in her office. He had his arms wrapped around her and a huge ring in his hand."

Omar shook his head. "You didn't learn anything from my mistake with your sister, did you? I can guarantee that whatever you *thought* you saw wasn't the truth."

Omar had jumped to conclusions when he thought Morgan had leaked her negotiating plans to the media. Had

Malcolm done the same thing? He closed his eyes and tried to conjure up the scene in Lauren's office, but the only image that he could see was Lauren in the arms of another man. After that, he'd lost all rational thought. "Why are you so sure?"

"Because I saw her at Siobhan and Justin's that night. She's in love with you." He hesitated, as if he were going to say more. "I promised Morgan I wouldn't say anything, but because you chose to act a complete idiot, I'm going to tell you. And if you breathe one word of it, I will kick your ass. Though I should do it anyway."

"Tell me what?" Malcolm asked impatiently.

"Lauren told Morgan that she loved you when they were in the kitchen."

"Why would she... Morgan doesn't even like Lauren, so I can't see Lauren her telling her the time of day."

"Morgan asked the same question. Lauren admitted it to Morgan because Morgan was the only one who believed she had ulterior motives where you were concerned. Basically, she wanted Morgan to know that she didn't."

Malcolm slowly lowered himself to a bench and buried his head in his hands. "She accused me of still not being able to trust her completely, of not letting go of the past." *And of breaking her heart.*

"And have you?"

"I don't know... I thought I had." What had he done?

"If you don't know, you'd better find out quick and decide whether you can live the rest of your life without her." A couple of players came in from the showers and dressed, their gazes straying to Malcolm and Omar across the room. Omar sat and the two continued their conversation quietly. "If you need to talk, you know where to find me."

Malcolm didn't want to talk to anyone except Lauren, but he had a team meeting in five minutes that wouldn't be over for the next two hours. He pushed to his feet.

Omar went to his locker and retrieved a duffel bag.

He frowned. "Where are you going?"

"Coach is letting me leave early. I want to go home and check on Morgan. She had a few contractions last night and two today, and I'm worried about her."

Malcolm's heart rate kicked up. "Call me if you end up taking her to the hospital." Granted, Morgan was a married woman now, but Malcolm didn't care. She would always be his baby sister, his twin.

"I will."

Malcolm went one way and Omar the other. It took all of his concentration to remain focused on the running back coach's voice. The only voice in his head was Lauren's. He had been angry that she'd assumed the worst without giving him the benefit of the doubt eight years ago, and it had taken him less than two minutes to do the same thing to her. He didn't have an excuse, aside from jealousy. From the first time Marcus had mentioned that a couple of guys were interested in Lauren, Malcolm had been scrutinizing every player's interaction with her. The fact that he'd seen Darren with his hands on Lauren more than once sent his mind to a place it never should have gone. And he couldn't very well ask her what her conversations with the players were about. Some players have personal health and diet issues that they would confide in Lauren about and it would be a breach of confidentiality on her part to discuss them with Malcolm.

He pulled out his phone and sent her a text asking if he could still come by after practice.

It took twenty minutes for her to reply with a one-word answer: No!

His chest felt like a three-hundred-pound linebacker was standing on it and he could barely breathe. He started to send another text but changed his mind. Meanings easily got lost in transmission, so he needed to talk to face-to-face. But when? If he went to her office tomorrow, she would probably throw him out, and he didn't want to risk someone hearing something and reporting it back to management. Saturday after the walk-through, he would only have a few hours before he had to report to the hotel. All players were required to stay at a hotel the night before a home game. Truth be told, he should probably delay the confrontation until after Sunday's game. He would be expected to be in full game mode and couldn't afford the slightest distraction.

But he didn't want to wait that long. His father's words rang in his ears: *A woman hangs in there for a long time deciding what to do, but once she decides to leave, she's gone for good. Don't ever let her get to that point if you love her.* His heart almost stopped. He couldn't take the chance that Lauren might close the door on them forever. *That* he wouldn't be able to handle.

Chapter 19

Sunday morning, Lauren checked in with the staff at the stadium to make sure the pregame, halftime and postgame meals, as well as refueling snacks, were prepped and ready to go. There was a bevy of activity in the locker room as the players took advantage of the spread Nigel and his team had laid out. The variety of fish and lean meats, brown rice, pasta, and vegetables would be instrumental in keeping their energy up. There were also sports drinks, pretzels, bananas and the like for halftime and throughout the game. She wished the players good luck and made her way through the crowd.

Lauren spotted Malcolm on the far side of the room. After the text he'd sent her on Thursday, they'd had no contact. He followed her movements but made no attempt to approach, which suited her fine. She was angry and hurt but would never do anything to interfere with his ability to focus. Doing so could get him injured, and despite everything, that would break her heart further.

Omar came to where she stood. "How are you holding up, Lauren?" he asked quietly.

She tried to put up a good front, but it was useless.

"Well, the good news is Malcolm is just as broken up."

She didn't know how that qualified for good news. "Oh?"

"Yep. Gotta go."

Lauren hazarded a glance Malcolm's way and found him still watching her with an intensity that heated her insides. Cursing her body's reaction, she spun around and left.

"Hey, Lauren. Wait up."

Her steps slowed as Darren jogged to meet her. "Hey, Darren. Ready for your big game?"

"You'd better believe it. I just wanted to let you know my girl said yes. We're getting married."

"Congratulations," she said sincerely. "I wish you two all the happiness in the world."

"Thanks. Are you and Malcolm okay?"

They were nowhere near fine, but she waved him off. "Everything's fine. You just focus on winning this game," she added with a little laugh.

Darren nodded. Someone called his name. He held up a hand, signaling him to wait, then told Lauren, "See you around."

Lauren gave him a wave and continued to her seat. It was the longest three hours of her life. The only thing that kept her from going completely insane was the fact that she had to monitor the players' hydration and energy levels throughout the game. The Cobras easily defeated their opponent, but on more than one occasion, she found herself ensnared in those piercing light brown eyes. How Malcolm spotted her in a crowd of seventy thousand people, she would never know. Not wanting to get caught in the mass of people at the end, she opted to leave with five minutes left on the clock. She'd already made sure the postgame shakes were ready, and they would be served by Nigel's staff.

Back in the safety of her home, she curled up on the sofa and cradled a small pillow in her arms. This was so much harder than last time. The love she'd had for Malcolm in college in no way compared to the deep grown-up emotions she experienced now. She'd held off telling her parents and calling Valencia, because she didn't want to tell them she'd failed again. But she needed to talk to someone.

As if on cue, her doorbell rang, and she froze. *Please don't let it be Malcolm.* She slowly made her way to the door and checked the peephole. Lauren frowned. What was Siobhan doing here and how had she gotten Lauren's address? She opened the door and found not only Siobhan, but also Faith and Lexia standing there with wide smiles. "Um…hi."

"Hey, Lauren. We heard my brother made an ass of himself, so we came to check on you," Siobhan said bluntly.

Faith held up a bottle. "We brought wine."

"And food," Lexia said, producing a medium-size gift bag.

Smiling for the first time in three days, she moved back and waved them in. "How did you find out where I live?"

Siobhan dropped down onto the sofa. "I have my ways."

Lexia laughed. "Honey, this woman can talk her way into anything. You don't even realize you've given up information until she's gone."

"Ain't that the truth." Faith lifted her hand, and she and Lexia did a high five.

Siobhan rolled her eyes, but she was smiling.

"Well, since you all went to the trouble to bring food and wine, we might as well dig in." The women followed Lauren into the kitchen. She filled glasses with the wine while Lexia laid out shrimp tacos with a cilantro cream sauce on homemade corn tortillas. "Lexia, you made the tortillas?"

"Yes. They taste so much better."

"And that sauce is to die for." Siobhan placed three tacos on her plate and spooned on a generous helping of the sauce. "Girl, I'm so glad you added this to the menu at the café." She turned to Lauren. "In case you don't already know, Lexia owns the café on the first floor of the building where our company is located. Before she took over, the only thing safe to have in that place was the coffee… *maybe*."

They all burst out laughing and took their food into the living room.

"So, what did Malcolm do?" Faith asked.

Lauren took a sip of her wine and then told them about what he'd walked in on. "The guy was thanking me for helping him with his weight-loss goals, which is my job, and showing me the ring he planned to give his girlfriend."

"Did you tell him that?" Lexia asked around a mouth full of food.

"No, because I shouldn't have had to. We had just spent the entire night together, and for him to think I'd turn around and do something like that…" She released a deep sigh. She noticed they were all staring at her. "What?"

"He spent the night here? During football season?" Siobhan had a stunned look on her face.

"Um…yeah." To Lauren's surprise, Siobhan burst out laughing. "What?"

"Girl, he'll be back. That boy has never, and I mean *never*, spent a night with a woman during the season. Most times he ends up breaking up with whoever he's dating before the preseason is over because he claims the woman is too clingy and he needs to keep his head clear."

"I found that all the Gray brothers are alike, Lauren," Lexia said. "They may mess up, but they're fiercely loyal to those they love and will make it up in the end. Khalil swore that he would remain a bachelor forever, too." She smiled knowingly. "You see how that turned out."

Faith chuckled. "And Brandon is worse. My baby has a bad habit of sticking his foot in his mouth, but I love him. And he's doing much better keeping both feet on the ground. Just like his brothers, all Malcolm needs is a good woman, and he's found that in you."

Siobhan undoubtedly knew her brother well, and Faith and Lexia seemed to believe he'd come around, but Lauren wasn't so sure. Not when he couldn't get past his trust issues. Her heart clenched with the thought of not laughing with him, playing their special card game or indulging in a *kissgasm*. But she didn't want to spend the rest of her life on eggshells with him every time something came up, wondering if he saw her talking to another of his teammates, or some other athlete if she decided to branch out. No, the best thing would be for them to end it now.

Malcolm had no desire to stand through the postgame interviews on the field, in the locker room and at the podium, but he stood there and answered question after question almost by rote.

Just when he thought it was over, he heard a reporter call out, "One last question."

He zeroed in on the familiar face of a man who wrote for a local newspaper.

"Rumor has it that you're dating the team's new dietitian. Can you confirm that?"

"Mr. Duvall, the only thing I can tell you about Lauren Emerson is that she is a team player and she brings a wealth of knowledge and experience that has already transformed our dining room. You saw our performance on the field today. We eat to win." With nothing else to say, he stepped down, and the quarterback took his place.

Malcolm kept going until he reached his car. For the first time in his life, he needed to get away from the football field. When he saw Lauren in the locker room earlier, he'd had a hard time not rushing across the room, hauling her into his arms and kissing her until they both reached a kissgasm, as she'd termed it. But the hurt reflected in her eyes had rooted him to the spot and nearly torn him apart.

It didn't help that he'd heard murmurings in the locker room about Darren proposing to his longtime girlfriend, making him feel even worse.

He had no idea how to go about apologizing and asking for her forgiveness, but he had to find a way. Omar had asked him whether he could live the rest of his life without Lauren, and the answer was a resounding no.

It was after five when Malcolm pulled into his driveway. His cell buzzed. He put the car in Park and dug the phone out of his pocket to read the text from Omar.

Need ur help. Morgan in labor. Won't go to hospital until she finishes Madden.

He replied: On my way.

Malcolm parked the car in the garage and hopped on his motorcycle. It would be easier to maneuver through the traffic and keep him from losing his mind with worry. That, as well as taking the surface streets, turned out to be a smart move, and he made it to his sister's home in less than twenty minutes. He'd barely stopped the bike and turned it off before he jumped off and rushed up the walk.

Omar answered the door less than ten seconds after Malcolm took his finger off the button. "Thank God," he muttered. "Please come talk to your sister. I'm about to pull my hair out."

Morgan yelled from the back of the house, "Hurry up so you don't mess up my game."

Malcolm shook his head and followed Omar inside. Morgan was seated on the edge of the sofa, her fingers moving deftly on the controller and eyes focusing on the large screen. "Hey, sis."

Her gaze left the game briefly to glower at Omar. "I'm still not going until we finish this game. And don't even think about trying to let me win. If you do, we're playing again." She groaned and sucked in a sharp breath as another pain hit.

"Baby, we can play as many games as you want when you get home," Omar pleaded. "Please, let's go to the hospital."

"Not until the game is over," she said through clenched teeth, breathing harshly.

Malcolm turned to Omar. "How far apart are the contractions?"

"About seven minutes."

Malcolm noticed that they were playing at the all-Madden level—the top and most difficult level, where the player could control all aspects of the game. He'd taught his twin how to play the game and was probably the only one who could still beat her most times. He hunkered down next to her. "Morgan, I need you to listen to Omar. Neither one of us knows anything about delivering a baby, and I'm not having my nephew born on the floor." He predicted the baby would be a boy.

"We could be almost done by now if the two of you would stop talking and play the game."

He gestured for Omar's controller. "You mind if I take Omar's place?"

She snorted. "No. You're still not going to beat me."

He laughed. "Girl, I can beat you with my eyes closed." They still had two minutes left in the third quarter and the five-minute fourth quarter to finish. "I tell you what, if I can score two touchdowns in the next two minutes, you go to the hospital."

Morgan paused the game. "And if not?"

"Then we finish it."

"You're on."

Malcolm took a moment to sub out two players then directed his full attention to the television. Within forty seconds, he'd scored a touchdown.

"Lucky," she mumbled.

He just smiled. Her team made it down the field to the

twenty-yard line. When her quarterback took the snap, his defensive end was on him before the quarterback's arm went forward, stripping the ball. Another one of his players picked up the ball and ran it in for a touchdown. Malcolm tossed his controller on the sofa. "Let's go."

They got her into the car, and Omar gave Malcolm a grateful smile. "Thanks."

"I'm right behind you." He donned his helmet, started up his bike and pulled out behind Omar's silver BMW. He worried the entire drive, especially when he saw Morgan slump over on the seat through the window. They couldn't get to the hospital fast enough for him. When they arrived, Omar stopped in the circular driveway in front of the emergency room entrance, hopped out and went around to Morgan's side. "I'll park it. Just get her in."

Omar tossed Malcolm his keys. "Thanks."

Malcolm watched Omar ease Morgan out of the car and slowly lead her toward the entrance. After finding a nearby spot for his bike, he came back, moved Omar's car and nearly sprinted back to the entrance. Inside, his steps quickened down the hallway. He entered the room just as Morgan was being lowered into a wheelchair. He hurried over. It killed him to see her in pain, and as much as he wanted to go back with her, that responsibility belonged to Omar now. It must have shown on his face, because Omar asked if he wanted to accompany them. "No. Just keep me posted. Do you want me to call the family?"

"Please. My parents are probably at the restaurant." They owned a family-style restaurant named after Omar's mother in Buena Park.

He had his phone out and was already dialing. He started with his parents, then called the restaurant and spoke to Omar's mother. Next, he sent a mass text to his siblings. He figured they'd all be descending on the hospital within the hour. Malcolm found a seat in the corner and rested his head against the wall. His heart still beat at an erratic pace, and he regretted not taking Omar up on his offer. He checked his watch again for fifth time. He resumed his position and prayed it didn't take too long.

After what seemed like an hour, he checked the time. Only thirty minutes had gone by. Malcolm didn't realize he'd been drumming his fingers on the arm of the chair until he met the frown of a woman sitting opposite him.

Malcolm clasped his hands together and drew in a deep breath in an effort to calm his nerves. If he reacted this way with his sister, he'd be a basket case when it came to his own wife and child. His own. Immediately, his thoughts shifted to Lauren. He missed his sunshine. And that's what she'd always been to him, lighting the dark areas of his heart with her love. He'd give up everything to be able to hold her in his arms again.

"Malcolm." His mother hurried over to where he sat, and he came to his feet. "Any word?"

He hugged her and kissed her cheek. "Not yet. They've only been back there about forty-five minutes. Hey, Dad." They embraced.

"How are you holding up?"

Malcolm's entire family knew how close he and Morgan were, and it didn't surprise him that his dad had asked the question. "I'd like to say I'm okay, but my stomach is in knots."

His father chuckled. "Wait until it's your turn."

The knot in his stomach tightened.

His mother studied him. She reached up and palmed his face. "Things aren't well with you and Lauren, sweetheart?" she asked knowingly.

He covered her hand with his own. "No. I messed up and I don't know how to fix it," he confessed.

She smiled gently. "I'm sure it'll come to you when you let go of all your past hurts."

Malcolm just shook his head. He never understood how

mothers always knew everything. But she had a point. He had to let go. He just needed to figure out how.

Minutes later, Omar's parents, Brandon and Faith, Khalil and Lexia, and Siobhan entered. The grandparents huddled together while Malcolm's siblings surrounded him.

After a round of greetings, Siobhan asked, "How did you get here so fast? You had a game today."

"Omar texted me right when I got home because Morgan wouldn't let him take her to the hospital until they finished their *Madden* game." He relayed how they'd been able to get Morgan out of the house. His brothers laughed.

"That girl," Siobhan huffed.

Everyone found seats, and conversation flowed intermixed with periods of silence. Three hours passed with no word, and Malcolm could feel his control slipping. He had to know how Morgan was doing. He jumped up and began pacing, then sat back down. His mother told him to relax because babies came on their own timetable. He tried, but his anxiety levels climbed as the hours passed.

At 2:30 a.m., Omar burst into the waiting room with a wide grin, and they all rushed over, clamoring for information. He held up a hand and waited until they quieted. "We have a healthy seven-pound, two-ounce baby boy. Mom and baby are doing fine."

Malcolm breathed a sigh of relief.

"Can we see them?" Omar's mother asked.

"She's asking to see Malcolm first, then we can visit a couple at a time."

Malcolm's family wasn't surprised by the request, knowing the bond between the twins. He could hardly contain himself as rushed down the hall. He stuck his head in the door of her room. "Hey, little mama."

Morgan rolled her head in his direction and smiled tiredly. "Hey. Come see your nephew."

He took slow steps to her side and stared in awe at the tiny baby snuggled in her arms. She lifted her son and Malcolm carefully cradled him in his arms. A rush of emotions engulfed him. "He's a handsome little dude. Looks just like his uncle Malcolm."

She laughed softly. "Mmm-hmm."

"What's his name?"

"We're naming him after Omar."

He wondered how it would feel to have a son who carried his name.

"Omar told me how you messed up with Lauren. Fix it, Malcolm. She loves you."

He stared into the eyes that were mirrors of his own. Even after several hours of labor and delivering a baby, she was still worried about him. "I'm not sure how."

Morgan gave him another small smile. "It's easy. Tell her what's in your heart. Don't be afraid, big brother. It's worth it."

"I love you, sis." Malcolm bent and placed a soft kiss on her forehead, his emotions rising.

"I know. Now give me my baby and get out of here. You need to get some sleep so you figure out how to get my new sister to the altar."

He chuckled and handed the baby back. She gave his hand a reassuring squeeze and closed her eyes. He quietly tiptoed out. He still didn't know how to fix the mess that was now his life, but he'd figure it out. Or die trying.

Chapter 20

It took Malcolm three days to get the courage to approach Lauren. Though he preferred to talk to her away from the practice facility, he guessed his best chance of her not sending him packing or not even bothering to open the door would be to start the conversation at work. He ate a quick lunch then sought her out.

Her office door was open, but she wasn't there. Sighing with frustration, he walked over to her desk to leave a note. He stared out the window for a moment, contemplating what to write. Then he saw her. She was sitting on one of the benches near the walking trail. He remembered her telling him how much she enjoyed the peacefulness of the area. For a moment, Malcolm observed her. The love he felt for her filled his heart and nearly overwhelmed him. When she'd wanted to keep them a secret and he hadn't, she'd risked her career to show him her love. She had been acknowledging her mistakes and trying to rebuild the trust between them little by little since the first day he'd seen her. Another wave of guilt assailed him. Steeling himself, he pivoted and strode out. It was now or never.

Outside, Malcolm slowly approached. The late summer temperatures were still near ninety, but the tree-lined trail provided some shade and relief from the heat. The closer he came, the faster his heart beat. When Lauren noticed him, she stopped eating whatever she had in the bowl and waited. He fully expected her to bolt, but she held his gaze fearlessly. "Hi."

"Hi."

He gestured to the bench. "May I?"

Lauren hesitated briefly before saying, "Sure."

He lowered himself next to her but said nothing for the first few minutes, taking time to savor her nearness. Malcolm leaned forward, braced his forearms on his thighs and clasped his hands. "You were right."

"About?"

"Me still holding on to the past. I honestly thought I'd let go, but seeing Darren touching you in the dining hall and then the hug and ring…it made me lose my mind for a minute. Jealousy, plain and simple. It's not an excuse, but it's the truth."

He glanced over his shoulder and found her watching him intently. He straightened. "I'm sorry for hurting you, Lauren. For not trusting you." Malcolm shifted to face her. He turned her face toward his, and the tears standing in her eyes caused his heart rate to speed up. "I love you, Lauren. I always have, and I trust you with my life, baby." He wiped the tear coursing down her cheek with the pad of his thumb. "Can we talk tonight? I need you in my life, and you'll never have a reason to doubt me if you give me another chance."

He opened her hand and placed the familiar ring box in the center. "I promise. Text me and let me know if it's okay for me to come over tonight." Malcolm leaned over and kissed her, and the sweetness poured into his soul. Rising, he went back the way he'd come.

He slipped into a seat in the conference room as the lights dimmed and the film started. An hour later, the lights came back on and the coaches spent the next while discussing what had gone well, what could have been done better and what changes would be implemented for the upcoming game.

On the way out, Malcolm called out to Darren and asked him to wait a moment. It was something he should have done before now, but pride had stopped him.

"What's up, man?" Darren asked when Malcolm reached him.

"First I want to congratulate you on your engagement. I wish you all the best."

The younger man smiled. "I appreciate that."

"And I want to apologize for my behavior last week in Lauren's office."

He waved him off. "It's all good. I didn't know you and Lauren were tight like that. Are y'all all right?"

Malcolm wished he could say yes, but it had been two and a half hours and she had yet to text him. "I don't know."

Darren clapped him on the shoulder. "It will be. Just wait. Lauren is good people and so are you." He extended his hand.

Malcolm smiled and shook the proffered hand. "And so are you. Thanks, man." He watched Darren saunter off, feeling a load being lifted off his shoulders. He left to go to the running back meeting. Now, if only things could go as smoothly with Lauren.

Lauren clutched the box in her hand, afraid to open it. It couldn't be. Yet when she lifted the lid, it was the same promise ring he'd given her in college. And the same one she'd tossed back. That he'd kept it all these years surprised her. She'd thought for sure he would have returned it for a refund, but he hadn't. She held it against her heart, closed her eyes and let the tears fall. She loved him and had been miserable without him the past week.

Her eyes snapped open. *I love you, Lauren. I always have...* His words came back to her in a rush. He'd never stopped loving her, even when she'd stopped believing in them. The ring was proof of that.

Lauren wiped her face, packed up the remains of her lunch and went back to her office, taking a side trip to the bathroom to check her appearance. For the balance of the afternoon, she read articles on the newest health and fitness developments that might benefit the players, but her thoughts were never far from Malcolm. After having to read the same paragraph three times, she set the iPad on her desk and rotated her chair toward the window.

Malcolm's confession played over in her mind, as did her Sunday afternoon conversation with Siobhan, Faith and Lexia. Aside from Valencia—whom Lauren had finally talked to and who had encouraged her to listen to Malcolm if he attempted to talk to her—she didn't have any other close girlfriends. And she could see herself becoming good friends with them. She opened the side drawer on her desk and took out the ring box. Opening it, she ran her hand over the small solitaire sitting atop a thin white gold band.

"I know it's not very big, but it's my promise to you. When I get my first NFL check, I'll replace it with a real engagement ring."

"It's beautiful, Malcolm, and I don't care about the size. Just you."

Malcolm kissed her passionately. "I promise to love you forever."

"And I'll love you forever."

And she would. Lauren picked up her phone to text him but changed her mind. She had a better idea. She packed up and went to wait for him.

When Malcolm saw her leaning against his bike, his steps slowed.

"I thought I could say it better than a text."

The corner of his mouth kicked up in a smile. "And what are you saying?"

"I'm saying I want you to follow me home." Before she could blink, he banded an arm around her waist, lifted her off her feet and slanted his mouth over hers. The kiss was one they both had been seeking—healing, restoration and renewed commitment. "Does that mean you're coming?"

Malcolm lifted a brow.

Lauren realized what she'd said and shook her head. "You know what I mean."

His eyes glittered with passion. "You sure? I'm down for both."

Sparks of desire shot through her veins. "I'm going to my car." She turned on her heel and strode to her car, his joyful laughter trailing her. She couldn't stop the smile curving her lips.

With traffic, it took almost forty-five minutes to get to her condo. Once inside, Malcolm stood with his back braced against the door staring at her.

"Why are you looking at me like that?"

"Do you have any idea how much I missed you?" He straightened and came toward her. "How much I missed talking to you, laughing with you?" He touched his lips to hers. "Kissing you? I need to hold you for a while. Can I do that?"

"Yes," she whispered. When he wrapped his arms around her and held her close, she laid her head on his chest and listened to the sound of his strong heart beating in her ear. In his arms, she felt sheltered and loved, and she couldn't imagine being any place else. They stood in the middle of her living room for the longest time, neither of them speaking. No words were needed.

Finally, Malcolm released her and, taking her hand, led

her over to the sofa. He stretched out and pulled her on top of him. He idly ran a hand up and down her back. "I don't think I've ever been so afraid in my life. Even when I was waiting for my name to be called in the draft, I didn't have this fear. I'm never letting you go, Lauren."

Lauren lifted her head and met his eyes. "That's good, because I'm never letting you go, either, angel eyes." They shared a smile. They fell silent for a short while, then Lauren asked a question that had been on her mind. "What happened to Carlos? I haven't seen him around."

"He was released."

"Do you know why?"

"The coaches don't let us in on their decisions. There were others who got cut, as well."

"Oh."

"I have a bye in two weeks. Will you go away with me for the weekend?"

"Where are we going?"

A mysterious smile curved his lips. "It'll be a surprise. Will you trust me?"

She knew he was asking about more than just the trip. "Absolutely." She resumed her position with a smile. Lexia had been right. Although Malcolm had messed up, Lauren believed he would more than make up for it.

"You're still not going to tell me where we're going?" Lauren fussed, sitting next to Malcolm in one of the airport cafés. She'd been anticipating the getaway since he mentioned it two weeks ago. Apparently, all of the players were looking forward to having the few days off, if the way they'd practically run out of the practice facility yesterday after their Wednesday morning practice was any indication. She'd heard a few players mention that they planned to spend time with family, but a good number were doing the same thing she and Malcolm were doing.

Malcolm sipped from his bottle of water and smiled.

"You can't hide it forever. We've been sitting here for almost an hour. What if we miss the plane? Shouldn't we sit near the gate?" He had already printed the boarding passes but wouldn't let her see them. And because they only had carry-ons, they'd had no need to check anything.

He reached over and silenced her with a kiss. "Relax, sunshine. You know I've got you." He glanced down at his watch and stood. "Let's go."

She hopped up, listening for the flight calls. She heard three different ones and frowned.

He laughed and stroked a finger across her lips. "This is supposed to be a vacation, so stop pouting."

He held her hand as they passed one gate after another. He changed directions abruptly and pushed through a crowd. There were too many people for her to see the sign as he handed their boarding passes to the man at the gate and started down the Jetway. The Delta logo was the only thing she saw. "You can't just cut in front of all these people in line," she whispered, taking furtive glances over her shoulder.

"I'm not cutting in front of anyone, sweetheart. It's our time to board." Malcolm gestured for her to go in front of him.

Lauren took one step onto the plane, then stopped so abruptly he almost plowed into her. "Wait. That means we're sitting in first class?"

"Yes. You're first-class, baby. Where else would I have you sit?"

"You are such a wonderful sugar daddy."

He laughed. "Get on the plane, woman."

The flight attendant who had been viewing the exchange with mild amusement said as they passed, "Honey, I wish I had a sugar daddy like him."

Lauren smiled. She'd never flown first-class, but as she settled into the large, comfortable leather seat, she mused she could get used to it.

Once everyone boarded and the safety information was given, the flight attendant said, "Sit back, relax and enjoy the one-hour-and-fifteen-minute trip to San Jose."

Lauren whipped her head in Malcolm's direction. "San Jose?" She'd only been to the city once. "The last time we came…"

"I thought it only fitting that we go back to the place where we first made a commitment to each other."

She threw her arms around him and kissed him with an intensity that left him breathing hard. "I love you."

"I love you, too." Malcolm leaned close to her ear. "But if you kiss me like that again, no matter where we are, we aren't going to stop until I make you—"

She clapped a hand over his mouth and hastily glanced around, hoping no one heard. "You are outrageous."

"*Me?* I'm not the one making up words like *kissgasm*."

"*Shh!* Somebody's going to hear you."

He chuckled. "You started it with that kiss."

Thankfully, the flight attendant came to offer drinks at that moment. They spent the remainder of the short flight talking. She told him about the visit she'd had from Siobhan, Lexia and Faith, and he shared pictures of Morgan and Omar's new baby boy.

When the flight landed, they deplaned, picked up the rental Malcolm had reserved and made the one-hour drive to Monterey. Despite check-in not being until four, the reservation clerk at the hotel recognized Malcolm and allowed them to move into their room an hour early.

Lauren went straight for the balcony that overlooked the water. Malcolm came up behind her a short time later and held her. She leaned against him and covered his hands with hers. "Thank you for this."

"Thank you for giving me another chance to get it right."

Lauren had never been more content. They only had three nights, and she wanted to make each one count. The first night they ate at one of the hotel's restaurants. When they got back to the room, Malcolm helped her work on her book and, afterward, they played another one of their special card games.

Friday, he took her to the Monterey Bay Aquarium. She couldn't believe that they spent over three hours looking at all manner of sea life. Her favorite, by far, were the jelly-fish. They drove to a park and walked around for a while. Then bought soft-serve ice cream cones, found a bench and sat by the water to enjoy them. The sun shone high in the sky, and the early October temperatures were in the low seventies, a ten-degree drop from LA.

Lauren leaned her head on his shoulder. "Can we stay here forever?"

Malcolm placed her arm around her. "I wish. This is going to have to hold us until the season is over. Though you'll still be working."

"Not as much. I can most likely do most of it by phone or email."

"How long is the lease on your condo?"

"A year. Why?"

He shrugged. "Curious."

She studied him, but his expression gave nothing away. Was he planning to ask her to move in with him? The only way she would do that was if they married, and he hadn't said anything that gave her any indication he was leaning toward that end. "What else do you have planned for this evening?"

"Nothing, besides dinner in about an hour and maybe another walk. Is there something you want to do?"

"No. I'm content just being here with you."

"Then we'll have to figure out a way to do this as often as possible."

After another few minutes, they went back to the hotel. She changed into the pink dress Valencia had talked her into getting when they had gone shopping. Malcolm changed into a pair of dark slacks and white dress shirt. They dined at Domenico's on the Wharf while watching the sun start its descent over the water. Lauren didn't think the night could get any better. She needed that second walk after eating so much. The crab-stuffed prawns were to die for.

Malcolm stopped the car at another stretch of beach, got out and came around to her side. "Are you okay to walk in your sandals?"

"If we're going to be on the sand, I'll take them off. It's not too cold."

"Okay." He took her hand, and they set off.

Halfway down the beach, she spotted what looked like a small house but realized as they came closer that it was a building where visitors could sit and enjoy the water. People could stand outside at the railing or sit inside when it was cooler. She climbed the steps and stood at the railing. The sky was an explosion of blues, oranges and reds, and palm trees swayed with the gentle breeze. Lauren turned and noticed that Malcolm still stood at the bottom. She walked over to the steps. "Are you going to join me?" Instead of answering, he took the steps two at a time until he stood on the one below her. He wore such a serious expression she started to worry. "Is something wrong?"

He lowered himself to one knee.

"Malcolm."

"Lauren, I have loved you since the first day you crossed my path in college. And even though we spent eight years apart, you've always had my heart. From this moment until I take my last breath, know that I will still be loving you, and only you. I promised you eight years ago that I would replace the promise with the real thing, and I'm here to make good on that promise, if you'll have me. Be my wife, baby, and complete my dreams."

He produced a black velvet box holding an emerald-cut solitaire—far bigger than the first one—with two rows of smaller emerald-cut diamonds flowing beneath it. Emotions clogged Lauren's throat for a moment, and she couldn't utter a word. She finally found her voice. "I would be honored to be your wife."

He removed the promise ring and replaced it with the engagement ring.

"Thank you for completing my dreams, too." There under the setting sun, they sealed their love with a kiss that promised forever. She couldn't wait to tell Valencia and her parents. Her dad was finally going to get those tickets.

Epilogue

Malcolm watched his beautiful wife of ten minutes smile and mingle with their guests and couldn't wait to get her alone. They had decided to get married right after the football season ended, when the Cobras had won the championship for the second time in three years. His mind went back the moment he'd spotted her while waiting in the gazebo that overlooked the mountains. She'd come to him on her father's arm in a sexy, strapless white creation that hugged the curves he loved so much. Her beauty had nearly knocked him to his knees.

"I can't believe all my babies are finally married. You and Lauren have made me so happy today. The family circle is complete. How long do I have to wait for grandbabies?"

Malcolm shook his head and chuckled. "Mom, you already have three, and with Lexia *and* Faith expecting, that'll be five. That's not enough to keep you busy for a while?" Even now as Malcolm stood listening to his mother, his eyes were following his stunning wife.

"Oh, I guess. And didn't Christian look so handsome and serious as the ring bearer?"

"He did." Christian fit in so well that it was as if he'd been born into the family. "I'm going to find my wife. Thanks for everything, Mom."

"Okay. I'm so proud of you." She patted his cheek and strutted off.

He made his way through the guests standing around talking while nibbling on the predinner appetizers and stopped to talk to his brothers and four cousins from Sacramento.

Cedric clapped him on the back. "I'm glad things worked out with you and Lauren, but now my mom is hounding me and Jeremy."

Jeremy took up the tale. "Yeah, she said, 'DeAnna has five children, and if they all can find spouses, surely the two of you can,'" he mimicked in falsetto.

Brandon and Khalil burst out laughing.

"Exactly," Lorenzo added.

Lorenzo's younger sister, Alicia, who had a two-year-old son and was eight months pregnant, shook her head. "Been there, done that. I'm done."

Malcolm wondered if something had happened, because she'd come to the wedding without her husband.

"Anyway," she said, coming up on tiptoe to kiss his cheek, "this is your day. Go find your beautiful wife."

He smiled. "I think I'll do that. Later." He spotted her talking to Valencia and made his way to her side. "Do you mind if I steal my lovely wife away for a minute, Lyn?"

Valencia smiled. "Not at all."

Lauren looked up at him, smiled and hooked her arm in his.

He led her to a secluded part of the garden. He'd been waiting all day to get her alone.

"What are you doing? We have guests."

"I needed a private place to kiss my wife."

Lauren's gaze flew to his. "I know you're not thinking…"

"Yep, that's exactly what I'm thinking."

"We can *not* do that here."

She started backing away, deeper into the garden, which was exactly where he wanted her. He closed the distance between them and kissed her possessively, his tongue sliding in and out of her mouth in a way that he knew would only have one result. He slowly gathered the material of her dress, lifting it higher and higher until he had it above her hips. He moved her skimpy lace panties to the side and pushed two fingers deep inside her, keeping rhythm with his tongue. Moments later, she flew apart in his arms, and a deep wave of satisfaction washed over him.

"I love you, angel eyes," she said, her body still trembling.

"I love you, sunshine." She was his first love. His last love. His only love. And from now until eternity, he'd still be loving her.

* * * * *

Don't miss other books in Sheryl Lister's
THE GRAYS OF LOS ANGELES *miniseries:*

A TOUCH OF LOVE
GIVING MY ALL TO YOU
PLACES IN MY HEART
TENDER KISSES

Available from Kimani Romance.

COMING NEXT MONTH
Available April 17, 2018

#569 IT MUST BE LOVE
The Chandler Legacy • by Nicki Night

Jewel Chandler's list of boyfriend requirements is extensive—and Sterling Bishop doesn't meet any of them. Sure, the wealthy businessman is gorgeous, but he also has an ex-wife and a young daughter. When steamy days melt into desire-fueled nights, Jewel wonders if he's truly the one for her.

#570 A SAN DIEGO ROMANCE
Millionaire Moguls • by Kianna Alexander

Christopher Marland, president of Millionaire Moguls of San Diego, is too busy for a personal life. When Eliza Ellicott arrives back in town, he knows no woman has ever compared. A broken heart gave Eliza the drive to succeed, and she's opened a new boutique. Can she trust him again?

#571 RETURN TO ME
The DuGrandpres of Charleston • by Jacquelin Thomas

Austin DuGrandpre never had a relationship with his father. Determined that his son—put up for adoption without his knowledge—won't suffer the same fate, he tracks him to the home of Bree Collins. The all-consuming attraction is unexpected, but when Bree learns Austin's true motives she faces potential heartbreak.

#572 WINNING HER HEART
Bay Point Confessions • by Harmony Evans

Celebrity chef Micah Langston's ambition keeps him successful and single. He plans to open a restaurant in his hometown—and that means checking out the competition. Jasmine Kennedy is falling for Micah until she discovers his new venture will ruin her grandmother's business. Has betrayal spoiled her appetite for love?

Get 2 Free Books,
<u>Plus</u> 2 Free Gifts—
just for trying the
Reader Service!

KIMANI™ ROMANCE

SPECIAL EXCERPT FROM

*Jewel Chandler's list of boyfriend requirements is extensive—
and Sterling Bishop doesn't meet any of them. Sure, the
wealthy businessman is gorgeous, but he also has an ex-wife
and a young daughter. When steamy days melt into desire-
fueled nights, Jewel wonders if he's truly the one for her.*

*Read on for a sneak peek of
IT MUST BE LOVE,
the next exciting installment in
THE CHANDLER LEGACY series by Nicki Night!*

A tap on her shoulder startled Jewel. She turned around and was
swallowed up by Sterling's piercing hazel eyes.

"Can I join you?"

Jewel's pulse quickened. She wanted to say no. She couldn't
control the effect he had on her. Despite that, she said yes. Sterling
eased his fingers between hers and they swayed to the music
together. Jewel felt as if she were back in school. Sterling had
never been the object of her affection then, but she felt something
brewing now.

Jewel physically shook her head to shake off whatever that
feeling was. She stepped back, adding space between Sterling
and her, then moved in time with the lively beat. Sterling matched
her step for step and before long they were engrossed in a playful
battle, stirring up memories of old popular dances. Next, a song
came on from their senior year. A certain dance was known to
accompany the rhythm. Jewel and Sterling joined the rest of those
on the floor, moving along with the crowd in unison. They danced,
laughed and danced more. Other songs began and ended and the
two were still dancing some time later. Dominique and Harper had
found partners, too, and were no longer beside Jewel and Sterling.

KPEXP0418

Sweat was beginning to trickle down the center of Jewel's back. Her body had warmed from all the movement.

"Whew! I need a break." Jewel panted, threw her head back and laughed. She hadn't danced that hard in years. She felt free. "That was fun."

"Let's get a drink." Taking her by the hand, Sterling led her off the dance floor and headed to the bar. He asked for two waters and handed one to Jewel. "Want to get some air?"

"Sure." Jewel took the ice-cold water Sterling had just handed to her. She moaned after a long sip. "I needed this."

Sterling took her hand again and led them to the terrace. Jewel was hyperaware of his touch as they snaked through the crowd, but didn't pull away. She liked the way his strong masculine hand felt wrapped around hers.

Once they hit the terrace, the cool air against her warm sweat-moistened skin caused a slight shiver. They maneuvered past people gathered in groups of two or three until they reached the far end of the terrace, which was lit mostly by the silver light of the moon. Jewel placed her hand on the marble parapet and slowly swept her gaze over the sprawling greenery of the country club and what she could see of the rolling hills on the golf course. Closing her eyes, she breathed in the fresh air, exhaling as slowly as she inhaled.

Sterling stood beside her. "Perfect night, huh?"

"Yes. It's beautiful. If my mother were here she would scrutinize every crevice of this place." Jewel turned to face Sterling and chuckled. "She's so competitive."

"So you've gotten it honestly."

"What?" Her brows creased. "Me? No."

Sterling wagged his finger. "I remember you on the girls' lacrosse team. Unbeatable. Let's not forget the swim team," Sterling added. "Didn't you make all-county, and weren't you named the scholar-athlete of the year?"

Jewel blushed. She'd forgotten all of that. "Well. Yes, there's that."

The two laughed and then eased into a sultry silence. Jewel and Sterling studied each other for a moment. The moonlight sparkled in his eyes. Jewel looked away first, turning her attention back to the lush gardens.

Don't miss IT MUST BE LOVE by Nicki Night, available May 2018 wherever Harlequin® Kimani Romance™ books and ebooks are sold.

Want to give in to temptation with
steamy tales of irresistible desire?

Check out **Harlequin® Presents®**,
Harlequin® Desire and
Harlequin® Kimani™ Romance books!

New books available every month!

CONNECT WITH US AT:

Harlequin.com/Community

 Facebook.com/HarlequinBooks

Twitter.com/HarlequinBooks

Instagram.com/HarlequinBooks

Pinterest.com/HarlequinBooks

ReaderService.com

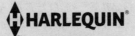

**ROMANCE WHEN
YOU NEED IT**

Need an adrenaline rush from nail-biting tales
(and irresistible males)?

Check out **Harlequin® Intrigue®**
and **Harlequin® Romantic Suspense** books!

New books available every month!

CONNECT WITH US AT:

Harlequin.com/Community

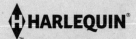

**ROMANCE WHEN
YOU NEED IT**

SGENRE2017

Reward the book lover in you!

Earn points from all your Harlequin book purchases from wherever you shop.

Turn your points into *FREE BOOKS* of your choice OR *EXCLUSIVE GIFTS* from your favorite authors or series.

Join for FREE today at **www.HarlequinMyRewards.com.**

Harlequin My Rewards is a free program (no fees) without any commitments or obligations.

MYR17